TO HAVE, TO HOLD

An Ever Green Romance

Darlene Polachic

From the heart for the heart

To Have, To Hold

Copyright © 2017 by Darlene Polachic

Formatted by Rik, Wild Seas Formatting (http://www.WildSeasFormatting.com)

ISBN: e-book: 978-0-9959518-0-8
ISBN: print book - 978-0-9959518-1-5

Chapter 1

They weren't going to make it.

The engine of the Jeep Grand Cherokee gave a sudden, sickening hiccup, confirming Janet Caldwell O'Grady's worst fear. The band of tension around her chest cinched tighter.

She clenched her teeth in frustration and steered the dying vehicle to the edge of the road. When fuel gauge said 'O miles to empty,' it wasn't kidding.

So close.

She'd hoped, prayed, they'd make it to her parents' home before the Jeep ran out of gas, but obviously that wasn't going to happen. The vehicle had guzzled more than the amount of fuel she'd assumed it would take to get from Sacramento to her parents' market garden farm in the community of Ever Green, east of Olympia, Washington. Mind you, she hadn't factored in the weight of the load. And while it didn't seem like they'd taken much with them (only the barest essentials) the truth was the SUV was jammed to the rafters.

Janet heaved an unhappy sigh because, no, the truth was something entirely different. The truth was that she'd put all the gas she could afford in the tank. It wasn't quite enough.

And as if to underscore that sad reality, the engine burped one more time and died.

Janet dropped her forehead on the steering wheel.

Now what, Lord? What do I do?

What she knew about vehicle mechanics could fit

inside a very small thimble, but even she was aware there was no point in trying to restart the engine. That would only run down the battery.

Worse, it was only a matter of time before the twins woke up and the circus began.

At six, the boys were well beyond taking afternoon naps, but after being hustled out of their beds in the dead of the night, the many hours of non-stop driving had lulled them into a deep slumber—for which Janet was deeply grateful. At least in sleep, the poor little fellows weren't conscious of their empty tummies. It was already mid-afternoon and they'd had no lunch.

Or breakfast.

If things had unfolded according to plan, they'd already be at Ever Green Acres where there was safety and food aplenty for all three of them. Instead, they were out of gas, stranded at the side of the road less than four miles from their destination, and visible for all the world to see, if by some chance they were being followed. They were totally vulnerable. Too far from her parents' home to walk the distance with two empty-tummied six-year-olds; just close enough for the bad luck of it all to taunt her.

"Are we there, Mommy?" Teddy's voice was husky with the remnants of sleep.

Janet twisted within the confines of her seatbelt and flashed a smile at her sandy-haired son. "Not quite, love. But we're pretty close."

In the booster chair beside him, Freddy blinked a couple of times and craned his neck to look out the window. "Where are we?"

Good question.

Janet did her own survey of the landscape. To a

stranger the surroundings might seem like one endless stretch of forest, thick with the evergreen growth typical of Washington State's coastal region. But even though this was her first time home in eight years, the terrain looked blessedly familiar. She supposed she should be thankful the Jeep hadn't stranded her earlier, because just ahead and around the curve would be Tireman Gas, known locally as The Tireman, where she would have to go if there was any hope of completing their flight to freedom. The practical aspects of visiting the gas station, however, made her insides convulse.

"Why have we stopped, Mommy? There's nothing here but trees."

The disappointment in Teddy's voice echoed the sentiments of her own heart. Janet O'Grady hated everything about the situation she and her boys were in. She hated the impossible circumstances, the sense of helplessness and profound vulnerability. They desperately needed a safe place to hide away, just for a little while, until she could consider her options and plan a course of action. She needed to find somewhere to start over and build a safe and secure life for her boys.

And she would. No matter what it took.

Janet brushed a unruly fringe of curls off her forehead, and for her boys' sake, feigned an animation she was far from feeling. "We've stopped here so we can go on a little adventure."

"Really?" Freddy, at least, seemed to catch the spirit. "I hope it has something to eat in it."

A lump clotted in Janet's throat at the note of longing in Teddy's voice. She swallowed with difficulty and frantically scoured her mind for something that might divert the boys' attention from their stomachs for just a little longer.

"Put your shoes on, my loves." She released her seatbelt with a flourish and pulled the keys from the ignition. "I'm going to show you something amazing."

"What is it?" Freddy's question was muffled as he scrambled on the floor for his sandals.

Janet made her voice sound mysterious. "You'll have to wait and see."

"I'm ready," Teddy declared.

"Me, too," said Freddy.

"You'd better have your sunhats, too. It's hot outside."

Janet tilted the side mirrors to make another inspection of the roadway behind them. She was probably being paranoid; there was little chance they'd been followed. But she'd be stupid to take foolish risks — —even though her only means of escape was stranded in plain sight like a beached whale. And what, after all, could she do if Bart O'Grady had seen her leave the Sacramento house at four in the morning, and had followed?

Not a thing.

Having determined that the roadway behind was clear, Janet opened the driver's side door and stepped outside, then moved quickly to open the rear doors to let the boys out.

After yet one more cautious look around, Janet ducked back inside and pulled her leather shoulder bag from its hiding place between a bag of bed linens and a box of the twins' Lego. She slid the purse strap high on her shoulder and clamped the body of the bag tightly under her left arm. Then, checking through the windows to make sure nothing of obvious value was in plain sight, she closed the door and pressed the remote to lock the doors.

Not that they had much of value left. Most of what she'd haphazardly packed into the Grand Cherokee fell into the absolutely necessary category.

It was ironic, Janet reflected, not for the first time. Anyone connecting her with this high-end sport utility vehicle would assume her money worries were few. But they'd be wrong. The truth was, she was a widow, the mother of two small boys, and penniless. Worse, she was on the run, and given the nature and desperation of the man pursuing her, she was quite possibly running for her life. Certainly, for her children's safety.

Janet grasped her boys by the hand and steered them toward the grassy verge on the opposite side of the road. "Are you ready to see something incredible?"

The boys nodded, and she set off at a jaunty pace, swinging their linked hands as they walked. To the casual observer, the trio might appear to have not a single serious care in the world, and that was exactly what Janet wanted. She'd made a fine art of putting on a happy face for her boys. Just because she'd made some stupid mistakes in her life and her world had been smashed to smithereens was no reason for her precious children to suffer any more than they already had.

* * *

Grant Brooks drove automatically, oblivious to the cedar- and hemlock-rich forest cover on both sides of the road and the scent of loam and evergreen wafting through the partially open window of his Lexus SUV. He generally loved this coastal environment, but today he scarcely noticed it. He was feeling strangely unsettled, unnervingly empty. Incomplete, somehow.

He'd been feeling this way a lot lately, though he couldn't put a finger on exactly why. It reminded him of the time he'd had a case of the mumps as a boy and been confined to his room. To pass the time, his mother brought him a puzzle she'd picked up for free at a thrift store because it didn't have a box. There was no picture to show how the finished puzzle would look, only a bag of pieces. Turned out the picture was a boy and his dog. The boy was holding something in his hand, but Grant never got to find out what the kid was holding because that crucial puzzle piece was missing.

That's how he felt now. As if an elemental piece of his life was missing. And he didn't know what it was or where to look for it.

Worse, there was no rational reason for him to feel this way. By most peoples' standards, he had everything a man his age could want. At 34, he had an enviable job as president and CEO of Ever Green Financial, a banking institution established by his great-grandfather in the early days of Washington statehood. His income was more than adequate to satisfy his needs, indulge his whims, and allow him to be as charitable as he wanted. His bank even had an unwritten policy of giving a break to worthy individuals that other financial institutions turned down on principle. There was a lot of satisfaction in that.

He had no family issues, though he sorely missed his beloved maternal grandparents, Pop and Gram Smith. When Pop died a few months ago, he'd left everything to Grant, including the gracious old home place in the Ever Green community. Grant had yet to decide what to do with it.

After his father died when Grant was a boy, his mother Maryann raised him, but they'd had a great relationship. Still did. A couple of years ago, she'd married Tom Forsythe—a fine fellow. They were both retired now, living in Palm Springs and enjoying traveling the world together. He and Tom got on extremely well, though Tom's over-the-top gifts sometimes embarrassed him. Like the Rolex on his wrist right now. Grant suspected the gifts were a subtle effort on Tom's part to win his favor, but there was no need for that. Any man who loved Grant's mom the way Tom obviously did and made her as happy as she obviously was, already had his full approval.

Grant glanced at the Rolex now to make sure he was on track for his 3 p.m. appointment.

Yup. The Tireman was just around the corner, so he'd be where he needed to be with time to spare. The meeting would be a quick one; all he needed was a signature from an elderly client on a document. On his way back to town, maybe he'd stop at The Tireman and say hello to Toni. Give her some business. Heaven knew she could use it.

Like he'd been telling himself, there was no reason on earth why he shouldn't be feeling on top of the world. As if the other blessings in his life weren't enough, he was engaged to a beautiful woman. A good Christian woman. Not head-over-heels in love the way Pop had been with Gram, but he admired and deeply respected this woman. He'd seen enough of life to know that not everyone experienced the kind of love his grandparents had shared, which was probably why he'd let the relationship drift along to the point where a wedding date was set and his bride-to-be was having the time of her life making the arrangements. He had no doubt the event would be stellar in proportion, but if that made his fiancée happy, that was fine with him. For his part, Grant had every intention of being a good and faithful husband to her.

"So what's my problem, Lord?" he inquired aloud, smacking his palm against the steering wheel. "Would You please show me what's missing and why I'm feeling this way?"

His introspection was interrupted by the sight of a vehicle some distance ahead, stopped at the side of the road with its hazard lights flashing. He automatically tapped the brake to de-activate the cruise control.

Seconds later, he noticed a woman walking on the grassy verge to the left of the paved roadway. There appeared to be two children with her.

Grant let the Lexus slow as he approached the parked vehicle. It was a newer Jeep Grand Cherokee with California plates. The interior looked to be packed full, but as far as he could see, there was no one inside which, given the temperature, was probably a good thing. It was unusually hot for mid-August in this part of Washington State. Too hot, certainly, to be walking any distance without the benefit of shade. Especially for little kids.

The woman was youngish, he could see as the distance between them diminished, with a wild cascade of curly dark hair spilling onto her shoulders. She wasn't wearing a hat, though the children were. Two boys, both about five or six, if he was any judge of such things.

Grant glanced at his watch again. His appointment was in ten minutes, but no business deal was more important than someone in trouble.

He pulled even with the trio and stopped, then frowned as the woman scooped her arms around the boys and brought them in close to her body, turning her back to Grant. The gesture reminded him of a mother hen hiding her young from danger beneath her wings. Her posture practically personified fear.

Grant lowered the window. "Hello," he called. "Do you need help?"

The woman didn't respond immediately, but Grant couldn't suppress a grin when two little-boy faces peered out at him from beneath her arms. Was he imagining a slight easing in the woman's posture?

After a moment's hesitation, she made a half-turn toward him.

She was slender, he noticed. Her dark hair swirled around her head in an unruly mop. But what struck him most were her eyes, which dominated her face. Even from this distance he could tell they were very dark brown.

He repeated his question, in case she hadn't heard him the first time. "Do you need help?"

The woman shook her head.

The little boys continued to regard him curiously.

"Are you sure? I'd be happy to give you a lift somewhere if you need one."

"We're fine."

He scanned the cloudless, sun-filled sky. "It's a hot day to be out walking..."

"We're fine," she repeated, the stiffness in her voice matching the hard angles that were once again ridging her shoulders.

Grant shrugged. "All right, then." If she wanted to be stubborn—stupid, even—how was that his business?

"Have a nice day."

He pulled away slowly, continuing to watch the trio in his rear view mirror until the road curved and they disappeared from sight. Something about them tugged at his heart. The woman denied needing help, but Grant knew better. In his line of work, he'd learned to read people pretty well and even this brief encounter had told him she was in some kind of trouble.

And she was terrified.

It showed in the hunch of her shoulders and the way she'd tried to hide the kids from his view. What would make her so fearful? An abusive relationship? Was she running from something? Or someone?

And why did he feel that he'd somehow failed them?

Maybe it was the children. Little kids always got to him.

Chapter 2

Janet waited until the metallic gold SUV disappeared around the curve in the road before tipping her head back and rolling it from side to side to ease the tension in her neck. The sound of its approach had petrified her. She was sure it was her brother-in-law, Bart. That he'd somehow seen them leaving the house in Sacramento in the middle of the night and followed. She'd felt totally exposed in the roadside ditch, totally vulnerable, totally foolish trying to hide in plain sight. What a relief to hear a stranger's voice.

Of course, she had no idea who the stranger was, and no assurance he wasn't someone Bart had put on her trail. But he didn't look like a thug. From what she'd seen of him, he was probably a businessman—clean-shaven, dark hair trimmed short. His voice was nice, and his concern seemed genuine enough. But she'd be a fool to take stupid chances. She had trouble enough already.

Teddy tugged at her arm. "What are we doing, Mommy?"

What were they doing?

They were standing in a roadside ditch. Which, like the stranger had pointed out, wasn't the best place to be on an overly hot summer day.

"We're going to see an incredible thing," Freddy reminded his brother. He peered at Janet from under the brim of his hat. "Will we see it soon, Mommy?"

"Very soon." They resumed walking again. "Why don't we play I Spy while we walk? You want to go first,

Freddy?"

"Sure," he said, and proceeded to look for a suitable object to spy. "I spy something that's black and white."

"A cloud," Teddy guessed, and was immediately treated to an explanation of why that answer couldn't possibly be right because clouds only had black in them when it was stormy and going to rain and today was a very sunny day.

"That rock." Teddy pointed to a boulder half-buried in the forest floor off to the side.

"Nope." Freddy tugged on Janet's hand. "Aren't you going to play, Mommy?"

"Of course I'm going to play. Let's see...black and white... How about the black pavement with the white line down the middle?"

"That's it. Mommy wins, Teddy. Now it's her turn to spy something."

If only she could spy a new life. Even a ten dollar bill at the side of the road would be helpful right now because how she was going to pay for the gas she needed to get the Jeep going again was beyond her. Janet knew for a fact there were no money bills in her purse. The best she could hope for was enough loose change to buy a portion of a gallon of gas from Mr. Cirelli, just enough to get her to the safety of her parents' home where her boys would be fed and have a bed to sleep in for the night. She'd figure out the rest after that.

An impatient tug on her arm pulled Janet back to the business at hand. She needed to spy something.

"I spy with my little eye..."

According to her calculations, The Tireman was just around the curve.

"...something that's mostly black and very, very

12

tall."

Two sandy-haired heads switched from one side of the road to the other and back again. "The top of that big tree," Teddy guessed.

"Nope."

There were several other guesses, and then Freddy spied a distinctive outline peeking above the tree line. "That?"

Janet gave his hand a congratulatory squeeze. "You got it."

If only the answers to life's problems came so easily. But when you'd made choices as foolish and life-altering as she had, easy answers were non-existent. She knew that from painful, first-hand experience.

By now Teddy had spotted the structure, too. "What is it, Mommy?"

"That's the incredible thing I want to show you. It's a giant man made from car tires. It's been there ever since I was a little girl."

"Who made it?"

"Mr. Cirelli, the person who owns the gas station."

"Will he be there?"

"I expect so."

She certainly hoped so. Janet remembered Mr. Cirelli as a kind and gentle man, a friend to everyone in the community. A man to be counted on when a person was in need.

Like the man who'd stopped a few minutes ago to offer help?

Janet swiped the perspiration off her forehead with the back of her wrist. He was right. The day was too hot for walking. Maybe she should have accepted his offer of a lift. For the boys' sake, at least. But after what she'd been through, she and trust were oceans apart.

A few minutes and a hundred questions later, Janet and the boys reached the clearing where the gas station and the towering man-o'-tires stood. While the twins inspected the structure, Janet studied the station. In some ways, The Tireman looked as needy and defeated as she felt. But at least the fuel pumps appeared functional. That meant the station was still dispensing gas.

"Come, boys. Let's go meet Mr. Cirelli."

Janet hoped Mr. Cirelli would remember her. Just as she hoped he still had that understanding, non-judgmental way about him. It would make it a whole lot easier on her pride when she asked for only a portion of a gallon of gas instead of breezing in like most of his customers and demanding a fill-up.

As it had been doing for decades, the bell on The Tireman's door jingled to announce their entry. Not much inside had changed. The cash counter was still to the right of the entrance, a display rack with packages of gum and candy on the front of it. Behind the counter sat a young woman wearing a Seattle Mariners baseball cap.

"Can I hel—?" The woman stared. "Janet—? Janet Caldwell?" She slid off the stool and rounded the counter slowly, as if unsure she'd made the correct identification.

"It's O'Grady now." Janet frowned. "Do I know you?"

The other woman laughed. "I should hope so. I'm Toni."

Janet blinked. "Antonia Cirelli?"

"In the flesh. I mostly go by Toni now."

Janet's chest tightened. Could things possibly get

more complicated? In their senior year of high school, she and Antonia Cirelli had both had a major crush on Marty O'Grady. In the end, Marty chose her. Or was it that Janet was the one foolish and willful enough to run away with Marty despite her parents' objections? Did Antonia hold that against her? How embarrassing it would be to beg a favor from Antonia Cirelli—who, at the moment, was giving her a thorough and unabashed perusal.

Toni had matured into a woman of quiet beauty. Her olive skin, a tribute to her Mediterranean roots, was flawless. Her perfectly arched eyebrows matched glossy black hair that was pulled back and fell in a graceful ponytail through the opening at the back of her ball cap.

What, Janet wondered, was Toni seeing as she stared back? The same rebellious brunette who'd given up everything, including her dignity and self-respect, to win Marty O'Grady? Or the reed-thin, stress-worn, twenty-six-year-old that she was? Neither image was particularly appealing.

"You work here?"

Toni slid her fingertips into the back pockets of her jeans. "At the moment."

"You were going to be a doctor."

Toni rocked a bit on her sneaker-shod feet. "Yeah, well, life doesn't always turn out the way we plan it."

Tell me about it...

"I started in medicine, but ended up training as a nurse because my grandmother was failing and I could see she'd soon need full-time nursing care. I graduated and immediately became Nonna's live-in nurse. She died four years ago. Now my grandfather needs the same kind of care, but he refuses to let me do it. He's opted to live in a care home so I can run the gas station, which hardly does enough business to stay open. But Nonno won't hear of letting The Tireman go." She gestured, palms upward. "So here I am. It isn't what I'd like to be doing with my life, but I feel I owe it to my grandparents. They raised me, after all."

Janet knew that, but had forgotten. "I'm sorry your grandfather isn't well." The news about Mr. Cirelli was disappointing on so many levels.

"Thank you. So am I." Toni drew in a deep breath, then deliberately shifted her attention to the twins who had been staring at her while she and their mother talked.

"These are your boys?"

Janet nodded. "This is Freddy," she put a hand on his shoulder, "and this is Teddy."

Freddy looked at Toni with knowing eyes. "I bet you're gonna ask if we're twins."

Toni raised a perfect bird-wing eyebrow. "Are you?"

"Yeah. We get that a lot."

"We're six, you know," supplied Teddy, ever loathe to be outdone by his twin. "We've finished Kindergarten. Now we're gonna be in First Grade."

The corners of Toni's mouth twitched. Laughter gleamed in the eyes that sought Janet's. "Your boys are delightful." She sobered then. "I heard about Marty. I'm sorry."

Janet nodded stiffly. She didn't want to talk about Marty. To anyone. And especially not to Antonia Cirelli. What she desperately wanted was to get home as quickly as possible, even though she had no idea what kind of reception she'd receive when she got there. It had, after all, been eight years....

But there was no way she was going *anywhere* without gas.

Janet pulled her purse around to the front of her and was opening it to see how much change she could find, when the service bell announced a vehicle pulling up to the pumps. Instinctively, she ducked behind a rack of shelving.

"Excuse me." Toni circled behind the counter again to set the fuel pump controller.

Janet used the moment to dig out her change purse. She snapped it open and peered inside. The contents would tell her how much gas she could afford.

It didn't take long to count. Six quarters, two dimes and a dozen pennies.

$1.82 — ?

It was all the money she had in the world.

* * *

Grant set the gas pump to fill and headed inside The Tireman. His appointment hadn't taken long, but he hadn't lingered, either. The picture of the woman and the two little boys trudging through the heat had stuck in his mind the whole time like a prickly burr. He'd taken the same route back toward town just in case the three were still out there. The Jeep was, but the hikers had disappeared.

Maybe Toni knew something about them.

The bell above the door jingled as he walked inside.

Toni was behind the counter. "Hi, Grant. You filling?"

He nodded. "Know anything about the Grand Cherokee parked up the road? It has California plates."

Toni shook her head.

"That would be mine."

He turned toward the speaker. It was the woman from the ditch.

She stepped from behind a row of shelving sparsely stocked with basic grocery items. Up close, she was a lot prettier than he'd realized. Creamy complexion, a little more sun-kissed than normal, thanks to the mile-or-so hike up the road, he figured. A tangle of cocoa-brown curls framed her face. Cute nose. And the biggest, brownest eyes he'd ever seen. At the moment, they were watching him warily, as if she didn't quite trust him.

"Did you have a problem?"

She shrugged and gave a light, self-deprecating laugh. "Would you believe I ran out of gas?"

Toni looked at her in surprise. "Janet, I'm sorry. I didn't even ask why you were here. Give me a minute to finish with Grant and then I'll look after you."

"There's no hurry."

Toni obviously knew the woman. Did that mean she was local? He couldn't remember seeing her before, though there was something vaguely familiar about her.

Grant shifted his attention to her boys. Twins, he decided. They both had round faces and sandy-brown hair that peeked below the blue denim sun hats they wore. Solid little boy bodies — the kind that made a person want to hug them tight.

At the moment, the two were sidling over to give the candy rack at the front of the counter some in-depth attention. One of them picked up a package of Smarties and studied it for a long moment. He turned it over. And turned it over again. He eased the flap up and peeked inside. Then, after a quick, guilty glance toward his mother, he hooked his forefinger inside, pulled out a bright yellow Smartie and popped it in his mouth.

Grant couldn't help grinning at the look of pure rapture on the little boy's face as he savored the candy-covered chocolate. His grin widened as he watched the boy hand the open box to his twin who also sampled the goods. They were little rascals, but off the scale for cuteness.

"Your boys?" he inquired, amusement coloring his voice.

She nodded, her mind clearly occupied with something else.

He stepped close — close enough for her hair to tickle his nose. "Looks to me like you've got a pair of junior kleptos on your hands."

She stiffened. Took a giant step away. "What are you talking about?"

Grant tilted his head toward the counter where her twin boys were now taking turns digging their fingers into a box of Smarties. Their jaws were working at top speed as if they meant to devour as many candies as possible before their sin was discovered.

Janet gasped, and addressed the one holding the box. "Fred-*dy*."

The sorrow-filled way she said his name made Freddy spin around, but not before he dropped the nearly-empty Smartie box back onto the display shelf as if it had suddenly become a burning coal. His face showed pure, unadulterated shame.

"I'm sorry, Mommy," he whispered and ran to hide his face in her shirt.

Janet drew him close and cupped the back of his head with a protective hand. "I know, sweetheart, I know."

His brother, tears pooling in his big brown eyes, looked equally remorseful. "I'm sorry, too, Mommy." His chocolate-smudged lips quivered. "But we're so hungry."

"I know, Teddy," she murmured and pulled him close, as well.

Grant felt like a world-class jerk. Clearly, there was more going on here than he knew. What he'd meant as something humorous was obviously deeply hurtful. And the last thing he wanted to do was hurt these little boys or their mother, whom he sensed already had more than her fair share of hurts.

His remorse deepened when Janet turned to glare at him, then reached toward the display case and snatched up the opened box of Smarties. She handed it to her sons. "Here, boys," she said, "finish them." She sent a defiant glance Toni's way. "I'll pay you for the Smarties."

Grant opened his mouth to instruct Toni to add the candy to his bill. It was a small thing that wouldn't nearly make up for his stupid remark, but at least he wouldn't feel like such a schmuck. But the way Toni was regarding Janet snapped his lips back together.

"No," she was saying to Janet, "you won't." She planted her hands on her hips and looked down at Janet's boys who were tipping the box on end to make sure they'd shaken out every last Smartie. "What you boys don't know is that whenever twins come to The Tireman, they each get a box of Smarties. Isn't that right, Grant?" The look she gave him defied him to dispute the statement.

"I'm almost positive I've heard you say that." Good for Toni; shame on him.

Toni plucked a brand new box of Smarties from the rack and handed it to Teddy. "Welcome to The Tireman. I hope you boys will come again."

"Thanks." A chocolate-gilded grin split the little boy's face from cheek to cheek. "I hope we can come again, too. Smarties are our favorites."

Toni gave him a wink, then leaned over the counter to consult the computer screen. "Your pump is done, Grant." She handed him the debit terminal.

Grant slid his card into the machine and tapped the appropriate buttons. As he waited for the transaction to finish, he looked over his shoulder at Janet. "Are you and your boys visiting in the area?"

She ignored the question. Probably not surprising given the way he'd embarrassed her. Served him right. Instead, she turned to Toni. "I won't need much gas..."

"I know. Just enough to get your vehicle to the station."

"Can you give me a dollar and a half's worth?" Janet counted out the appropriate change.

Her fingers weren't quite steady as she placed the coins on the counter, Grant noticed as he accepted his transaction receipt from Toni.

"Why don't you wait and pay me when we've filled the tank?" Toni suggested.

"No." Janet's voice was firm. "We'll do it this way."

Toni shrugged. "If that's what you want." She crossed to a storage cabinet and brought out a red plastic gas can.

The woman was broke. Grant knew it as sure as he knew his own name. He'd seen that look on people who came to the bank desperate for a loan. Someone had once described it as feeling like a thin-shelled egg rolling toward the edge of a slanted table. That's exactly how she looked. Something inside made him want to keep her from crashing over the edge.

"I've a suggestion. Toni, you and I can take the gas to this lady's vehicle. We'll get it started and you can drive it back here for her." He looked at Janet. "That way you and your boys won't have to walk again in the heat."

"Great idea," Toni declared. "Let's do it."

Grant headed for the door, not waiting for Janet's approval or permission. If he did, she'd probably refuse. He knew her type. She was in some kind of trouble and too proud to admit it. Too proud to ask for help.

Chapter 3

The last thing Janet wanted was to be beholden to Toni or this Grant fellow, but she had to admit, his suggestion had appeal. If there was a trick to getting a vehicle restarted after it had run out of fuel, she certainly didn't know it.

"I appreciate this," she said stiffly, handing Toni her car keys. "The boys and I will wait outside in the shade." The eloquent glance she directed toward the candy rack spoke for itself.

Toni frowned. "Don't be ridiculous, Janet. Grant's right. It's far too hot out there. You'll be much more comfortable inside where it's air conditioned. In fact—" she ducked behind the counter and emerged a few seconds later with some paper and a plastic cup of crayons "—would you boys be interested in drawing a picture of the tireman for me? I've been thinking about putting up some art in the station."

The boys eagerly accepted the paper and crayons.

"Oh," Toni added, "if a customer comes in while I'm gone, tell them I'll be back in a flash. Okay, boys?"

"O-*kay*," they chorused.

"Make yourself at home in my office, Janet." Toni nodded toward a room at the back. "There's juice in the fridge and fresh coffee. Please help yourself to whatever you'd like." And with that she, too, headed out the door.

The back room proved much more aesthetically pleasing than the business end of The Tireman. It contained a walnut desk, a pair of upholstered easy chairs, a television and a bookcase stocked with paperbacks and magazines. There was also a spacious coffee table that the twins immediately claimed as their own and set to work on their tireman masterpieces.

Janet located some juice boxes in the little bar fridge and gave one to each of the boys. She hadn't intended to drink Toni's coffee, but the aroma was more than she could resist. All she could find to hold it were pretty china coffee mugs, so she filled one with the fresh brew and added a dollop of the cream she'd spotted in the fridge. Cradling the mug in both hands, she sank into one of the easy chairs and took a long sip.

Her chest still burned with resentment toward that Grant fellow. How dare Mr. Designer-Suit-Silk-Tie judge her boys? What right had he to infer they were habitual thieves? —Her beautiful, innocent little fellows whose hearts were bigger than the states of California and Washington combined. This man knew nothing of what they'd been through. Of what they were still going through. She was willing to bet he'd never once in his life known real hunger, as her boys had. Why, the price of his Italian shoes alone could keep her and her boys in groceries for a month.

Maybe two.

But beneath her resentment was awareness, too. No matter how much she wanted to despise him, there was no denying his physical appeal. Crisp dark hair with just a hint of a curl. An angular face with a strong square jaw. Nice nose, though it had a hint of a hump at the bridge. His eyes were the deep greeny-gray of a stormy sea—

Good heavens... How had she noticed all that in the brief moments she'd spent in his company? More important, why *would* she notice? The fact that she had noticed made her all the more resentful.

She sighed and leaned her head against the upholstered chair back. Her head ached. Her shoulders ached. Her whole body ached. She knew it was from a combination of things: lack of food, the long tense drive, weeks of stress and uncertainty since Marty's death, her brother-in-law Bart's bone-chilling threats, worry over what lay ahead...

Janet drew a ragged breath. She was trying to put the worry aside, to allow God to work things out, but it wasn't easy. When you made bad personal choices, it seemed reasonable to believe God would pretty much say: "It's on you, kid. You made the decisions; you live with the consequences." She knew in her heart that God wasn't like that, but some days — like today — it certainly felt like He was.

She could just imagine what Toni was telling Grant about her right this minute. How she'd run off with the local bad boy, estranged herself from her family, and was now reappearing out of the blue. Seeing the Jeep packed to the ceiling with their personal belongings would give the unmistakable hint that all was not well in her world, and that she wasn't just home for a brief visit.

Could things get any more humiliating?

Janet closed her eyes, hoping to mitigate the throbbing inside her skull. The chatter of her boys soothed the raveled ends of her nerves. At least they were content...

She awoke to the distant sound of a tinkling bell.

Seconds later, Toni was standing in the doorway. "You're good to go, Janet."

She stepped inside to inspect the twins' drawings.

"These are very good, fellows. I'm going to put them on the wall right away." She ran a finger across the oversized and sometimes backwards lettering. "I'm glad you signed your names."

The boys beamed.

Embarrassed at being caught napping, Janet placed the empty coffee cup on the table and stood. Looping her purse strap over her shoulder, she ushered her boys toward the door. "Thanks, Toni, for the coffee and juice...and everything. It was great seeing you again."

Toni stopped in the doorway. "If you're going to be around for a while, Janet, I hope you'll drop in for a real visit."

"I might just do that." *Or not.* "Thanks again."

She hustled the boys outside and into the Jeep before Toni could bring up the awkward matter of filling her gas tank.

A mile down the road, she discovered why Toni hadn't.

Her gas tank was already full.

* * *

Grant eased back in his office chair and absently twirled a pen between his fingers.

Christa's sister — ?

Janet, the woman in the ditch, was his fiancée's sister?

That's what he'd learned from Toni on the way to Janet's stranded vehicle. And that's about all he'd learned, other than that Janet lived in Sacramento and had recently become widowed.

Why, he wondered, had he heard nothing about her or her situation from Christa? Though, in his fiancée's

26

defense, he was sure somewhere along the line of their four-year acquaintance she might have mentioned having a young sibling because Grant had the impression they weren't close.

He'd never given it a second's thought. Lots of families had complicated dynamics. But having met Janet, and seen the hunted look in her eyes, the fact that the sisters weren't close made him... Sad, was the only way he could describe the way he felt. Janet looked like she could use a friend.

A knock on Grant's office door prefaced the appearance of his secretary who entered and crossed the room to place a large envelope on his desk. "These papers are ready for you to sign, but you might want to give them a once-over first."

Grant uncapped the pen he'd been rolling and pulled several paper-clipped sheets from the envelope. "I trust you, Dorothy. I've yet to find you've made a mistake."

The gray-haired matron smirked, but Grant could tell his statement pleased her. "There's always a first time, boss."

He located the lines requiring his signature and signed with a confident scrawl.

"Thanks." Dorothy scooped up the pages and slid them back in the envelope. "I'll get this in the afternoon mail."

Grant rested his palms on the desk top and looked up at his secretary. "How long have you lived in Ever Green, Dorothy?"

She tapped the bottom edge of the envelope to settle its contents. "About six years. Why?"

Six years... He'd moved to Ever Green from Seattle

to take over the family's banking enterprise, Ever Green Financial, when his paternal grandfather passed away five years ago.

"Do you know Janet Caldwell?"

Dorothy looked thoughtful. "I think I've heard the name. It seems to me Bill and Verna Caldwell have another daughter." She pinned him with a look. "But you'd know more about that than me." She tucked the envelope under her arm. "What about her?"

Clearly, he wasn't going to get insider information from this source, which was fine with him, because the last thing Grant wanted to hear was gossip about Janet. And he had the uncanny feeling that she might very well be the object of gossip. There were so many things that didn't add up.

"She's back in Ever Green."

Dorothy raised her carefully drawn eyebrows. "For a visit?"

"Probably."

"Nice." Dorothy pointed to the envelope. "I'll look after this."

Grant was scarcely aware of the office door closing, because for some reason, Janet Caldwell Whatever-Her-Married-Name-Was was determinedly stuck in his mind. Probably because so many things about her didn't ring true.

For instance, she drove a pricy SUV but didn't have the price of a gallon of gas in her purse. He'd seen her counting out the coins. He'd also seen the panic on her face when he'd drawn her attention to her boys devouring the Smarties. And speaking of the boys, he felt like a first class jerk. They weren't being brats. Those kids were hungry, and their mom was too broke to feed them.

She was also running. Given the fact that the Jeep was packed to the rafters with personal effects, it was safe to assume hers was no brief family visit, as he'd let Dorothy believe. So was Janet coming home to her family hoping to be received with open arms? He certainly hoped she would be, but given that he and Christa had dated for three years and he'd never heard her name mentioned once...

And Janet was scared. Any idiot could see that in the way she'd tried to shield her boys from view there in the ditch. Which made him wonder: What was she hiding them from? Several scenarios came to mind and he found he hated every one of them.

A hint of a smile curved his mouth. The way she'd dealt with her boys over the regretful Smarties episode tugged at his heart. She reminded him of a mama bear defending her cubs. The sight had roused his protective instincts and made him want to sweep Mama Bear and her cubs into his arms and promise he'd keep all three of them safe.

Grant tossed the pen onto the desk top.

He'd never felt this way before. And that troubled him, because the response was totally inappropriate. He was on his way to the altar with another woman.

Even more troubling, the other woman was Janet's sister.

Grant frowned and shook his head. What was the matter with him?

It must be those winsome little kids who'd messed with his head. Whatever it was, he felt like he'd been t-boned, which made no sense. It was really none of his business.

He slid a short stack of files toward him and went to work.

Chapter 4

Janet pressed a hand to her stomach to quell the sick feeling there.

Someone had filled her gas tank. She didn't know if it was Mr. Look-At-Me-I'm-Rich Grant, or Antonia Cirelli who'd recognized her poverty and taken the hit, but either way, it was humiliating.

Face it, she hated being poor.

Unfortunately, that was her new reality.

But it wouldn't be for long, she vowed, reclenching her hands on the steering wheel. One way or another, she was going to climb out of her financial abyss and make a life for herself and her boys if she had to do it tilling gardens with a table fork.

Janet drew in a lung-deep breath and expelled it in a noisy whoosh. So much depended on what happened in the next few minutes. Would her parents welcome and accept after the rebellious and cavalier way she'd treated them? Would they allow her and her boys to hide away with them until it was safe to re-emerge? The uncertainty only added to her angst.

The turn-off to the farm was just up ahead. First there would be the big carved wooden sign at the corner of the lane announcing Ever Green Acres. Then there'd be the lane with its double row of trees, exquisitely colorful when the crisp autumn temperatures turned the leaves to ravishing crimson and glowing gold. Now, of course, the trees would still be in full leaf, almost linking branches above the laneway, their lush greenery creating a shady canopy.

Janet slowed the Jeep to a crawl, taking in the details. The sign, she noticed, was somewhat overgrown with blackberry brambles. Her father had always taken inordinate pride in keeping things around the farm looking trimmed and tidy. He was falling down on the job.

She turned into the long laneway and let the vehicle's momentum carry it forward at a snail's pace.

"Is this where our grandma and grandpa live?" Teddy inquired.

"This is where they live." Her voice was cheerful, unlike her heart.

What if her parents rejected her?

As she deserved. As she'd rejected and dismissed them.

"Will we meet them soon?"

"Very soon."

Janet's roiling stomach knotted tighter. Her parents would be seeing their only grandchildren for the very first time. She'd sent a birth announcement nearly seven years ago to herald their arrival, but she hadn't called since. Never brought the twins for a visit. Nor had she invited her family to visit in Sacramento. She'd wanted to, had longed to make amends and re-establish a relationship, but Marty forbade it. Didn't want anyone messing in his business, he said. Did her parents resent not knowing their grandchildren? She wouldn't blame them if they did. The estrangement wasn't their fault. It was entirely hers.

A grapefruit-sized lump of regret blocked her throat.

Please, God, give me courage...

The Jeep rolled to a stop where the tree-bordered lane opened onto a large open space. To the right were the first of the market garden plots, row upon row of vegetables stretching almost as far as she could see, waiting to be harvested and the produce sold at market. Beyond that was the orchard. On the left was the three-bedroom ranch-style bungalow in which she'd grown up. It looked more worn than she remembered, as if it too was feeling its age.

Mindful of the need for obscurity, Janet pulled the Jeep to the far side of the parking pad where it couldn't be seen from the highway.

As she turned off the engine, she noticed movement at the kitchen window. Her mother?

She drew a deep breath. "Ready, boys?"

More important, was she ready?

She pressed the switch to unlock the doors.

Freddy and Teddy had their seat belts unfastened and were out the vehicle in a flash, lured by open space where they could run as far and as fast as they wished.

Janet followed more tentatively.

The screen door of the farmhouse opened. Her mother stepped out, looked at the two little boys who were already chasing one another around the Jeep. Shifted her gaze to the young woman standing uncertainly beside the open driver's side door.

Nervousness glued Janet's feet to the ground and her tongue to the roof of her mouth. Did her mother not recognize her? Or was her presence unwelcome? Was her mom wondering why, after eight long years, her rebellious, runaway daughter had finally come home?

Verna Caldwell frowned. "Janet — ?"

Her mother's voice held disbelief — and something

more. Something that sounded like raw hope. Whatever it was, it had the effect of thawing Janet's frozen limbs. She moved swiftly toward her mother. "Hello, Mom."

"You're home..."

The twins abandoned their play and came to stand on either side of their mother. They studied the older woman with curious eyes. "Are you our grandma?" Teddy was bold enough to ask.

Verna Caldwell's gaze took in one twin, then the other. Her eyes welled with moisture and her smile wobbled.

"Mom, these are my sons." Janet introduced them. "Boys, this is your grandma."

Verna hesitated, as if unsure what to do or say, but Freddy had no such reservations. "Oh goody. We've never had a grandma before."

Verna shot a delighted glance at Janet, then lurched forward to clasp her daughter and her twin grandsons in one enthusiastic group hug. Tears trickled down her cheeks.

Freddy was the first to wriggle out of his grandmother's grasp. "You're dripping on me, Grandma. I'm getting wet."

Verna pressed a hand to her mouth to stifle a hiccupping laugh.

Teddy made his own escape. "Do we have a grandpa?"

Their grandmother beamed and clasped her hands together under her chin as if she couldn't trust herself not to crush the twins close again. "Oh, do you *ever* have a grandpa! He's inside taking a nap, but he's going to be *so* excited to meet you two."

"Will he play with us?" Clearly, Freddy considered

this primary among desirable grandfatherly qualities.

"I'm sure he will."

Janet listened with only half an ear to the conversation. Her father was having a nap? Her father never napped, especially in the afternoon and at the height of market garden season. She touched her mother's arm. "Is something wrong with Dad?"

Verna gave a little shrug. "We'll talk about that later, dear. I'm just so glad you're home. Let's go inside."

Teddy tugged at his mother's arm. "Can me and Freddy play outside, Mommy? Please?"

"As long as you stay out of the garden." Janet frowned. "But wouldn't you like something to eat first?"

Teddy gave the matter only the briefest thought. "I'd like an apple. Would you like an apple, Freddy?"

His twin nodded, though his eyes remained fixed on the grassy expanse behind the house.

"There are some lovely apples inside. Janet, why don't you go in and get a couple? They're in the yellow bowl on the kitchen table." Verna turned back to the boys. "I hope you boys have big appetites, because I have a chicken roasting in the oven. We're having company for dinner."

Janet pushed aside a flicker of annoyance at that bit of news and headed inside for the apples. She'd hoped to give an accounting of herself with only her family present.

In the kitchen, the savory aroma of roasting chicken sent a tidal wave of digestive juices sloshing in her stomach, reminding her how long it had been since she'd eaten.

Little had changed in the eight years she'd been away. The white refrigerator still made that odd buzzing noise, and the stove hadn't lost the rust spot on the bottom drawer that she and Christa declared was a perfect replica of their school principal's profile. Poor Mr. Griswald... Even the old rooster with the clock face in his stomach was still marking the seconds with a flick of his emerald green tail. The boys were going to love him...

As her mother had instructed, shiny red apples were mounded in a sunshine yellow bowl on the kitchen table. Janet quickly scooped up two for the boys and a third for herself and headed back outside.

In some ways, she felt like the biblical Prodigal Son. She'd come home at the end of herself, full of dread, uncertainty, and — yes — plenty of shame. She'd received a welcome she neither deserved nor expected. At least from her mother...

She had yet to encounter her father.

And her sister Christa.

The twins were racing on an imaginary track around the perimeter of the lawn and paused only long enough to snatch an apple from her hand as they flew by. Their shouted thanks rippled on the warm summer air.

An impossibly wide smile lit Verna's face as she watched her grandsons streak away, their little boy heels kicking up behind them like young colts'. "Your dad is going to adore those boys."

"Tell me about Dad." Janet took a bite of apple and watched her mother's expression shift from delight to sadness.

Verna wrapped her arms around her middle. "Dad's been very tired lately. The doctor says it's his heart. Says he needs to take it easier." Her eyes scanned the vegetable plots. "That's not so simple at this time of year."

Janet knew what her mother was saying. At the
height of production and harvest, it was all hands on
deck. She remembered the many hours she and Christa
had spent in the garden as teens. Who helped with the
work now, she wondered? Was her mother picking up
the slack? Maybe that accounted for the silvery streaks
in her hair and the new lines in her face? And on top of
everything else, her mother was cooking for company..?

"Who's your dinner company?"

"Oh, just—" Verna broke off to follow the progress
of a vehicle that was turning in at the far end of the lane.
"There's Christa now. She'll tell you all about it." She
gave Janet's arm an apologetic pat. "I need to get back
inside and check on the chicken."

Janet finished her apple and tossed the core beneath
a birdfeeder suspended from a tree. The robins would
make short work of it. Licking the juice from her fingers,
she followed the approach of a little white sports car.
Trust Christa to drive a vehicle that impressed.

Would Christa be as welcoming as their mother had
been, Janet wondered? Or would she be resentful of her
kid sister's return? She and Christa had never been close
growing up though there was little more than a year
separating them in age.

Christa was the older daughter, the one who'd made
few ripples. She was the type who calculated every
action to avoid making mistakes. Christa liked things
structured and predictable, the ultimate organizer. Janet
had always been the impulsive child, inclined to resist
guidance and make reckless, spur-of-the-moment
decisions. Some had dragged her into deep trouble,
exactly the kind of trouble that had kept her estranged

from her family all these years.

The little white car rolled to a stop near the Jeep. It was a Miata, Janet realized. She could see Christa giving the Jeep a long look. Had she noticed the California plate? Would she put two and two together?

The door opened and her sister swiveled in the seat and gracefully swung her long legs out of the car. Christa was also the glamorous Caldwell sister. Tall, long legs, classically beautiful features. Long-lashed eyes that owed nothing to extensions. White-blonde hair that fell in a sleek pageboy with the ends curling inward to caress the slope of her shoulders. Wonderful aquamarine eyes that were, at this moment, impossibly wide and glued to Janet's face.

"Janet—?"

A second later, Janet found herself wrapped in a fragrant hug.

Over her sister's shoulder, she saw her own unremarkable reflection in the car window. Her unruly curls were badly in need of a cut. Her chocolate brown eyes were probably her best feature. She had fullish lips—too full for real beauty, she'd always felt. The face she saw reflected was pleasant enough, but next to Christa's, it looked singularly uninteresting.

Not that any of that seemed important to her sister who was holding her an arm's length away.

"What on earth are you doing here?"

Good question....

"I've come home."

"It's about time."

Janet sighed. "I know."

Christa's arms dropped, suddenly aware of childish squeals from the twins who were still chasing each other around the yard. She pinned Janet with a questioning look. "Yours?"

Janet nodded and waved the twins over. "Boys," she called, "come and meet your Aunt Christa."

Freddy and Teddy screeched to a stop long enough to say hello, and then were off again.

Janet watched them go. The warmth of her mother's and Christa's welcome was helping her to set aside the unhappy incident at The Tireman and the humiliation she'd endured at the hands of Grant Whatever-His-Last-Name-Was, and for that she was grateful.

She turned back to Christa, taking in the taupe-colored linen dress that skimmed her sister's slim figure and the tasteful aquamarine jewelry that made Christa's eyes look like gemstones themselves. In her own crumpled capris and tee-shirt, she felt very much the poor relative. "You were at work?"

Christa nodded. "At the downtown library."

Janet chuckled. "No surprise there."

Christa gave an elegant little shrug. "I mostly do administrative work and event organizing. I worked in a school library for a while, but I discovered I'm not good with children."

Janet wrapped her arms around her waist. "What's the deal with Dad, Chris? I mean, it's nearly four o'clock in the afternoon and he's taking a nap? What's up with that?"

Christa shook her head slowly, causing the tips of her hair to brush against her throat. "Dad's not doing very well."

"Mom said it's his heart."

"It's been bothering him for quite a while."

There was no censure in Christa's statement, but

Janet couldn't help wondering if worrying about her had contributed to her father's condition. "Who does the field work?"

"Mom and Dad have a couple working for them."

"Can they afford it?"

"They can't *not* afford it."

Well, that would change, Janet decided, now that she was home. She wasn't afraid of hard work, and she was more than willing to help out. She'd work for a pittance—for nothing, even—in exchange for a safe place for her boys. At least until she came up with a plan for how to proceed.

"I'm surprised you're still living at home."

Christa shrugged lightly. "It helps Mom and Dad. I pay them for room and board."

The sick feeling renewed itself in Janet's throat. *She* couldn't contribute a cent. Maybe coming back to Ever Green wasn't such a smart move after all.

"I'm sorry about Marty."

"He was cheating on me, Chris. He was with another woman when he died. And she wasn't the first."

Christa didn't appear shocked. "Mom and Dad warned you."

Janet's jaw tightened. Not exactly sympathy... She probably wouldn't be telling Christa how she'd been little more than a glorified housekeeper for the past seven or so years, cleaning and maintaining the mansion that Marty liked to show off to potential investors in the business he and his twin brother Bart ran. Marty would bring the customers to the house, serve them cocktails and deliver the spiel about how he could make them all as wealthy as he was. Some gorgeous young nymph in a thigh-high skirt and ridiculously high heels would distribute the fancy *hors d'oeuvres* Janet was required to prepare. She'd noticed that Marty's clients tended to be young neophytes to the world of investment who were suitably impressed by all that Marty O'Grady had amassed and were easily convinced that this, too, could be theirs. That wealth was only an investment (with him, of course) away.

"We'd have come for the funeral if you'd let us know when it was."

"There was no funeral." Janet met Christa's look squarely. "I didn't feel there was much to honor. It wasn't a good marriage. And you're right. Running away with Marty was the biggest mistake of my life. I'll regret it to the day I die."

Christa reached over and squeezed her arm. "It wasn't all a mistake. You have your boys."

Janet gave a shaky laugh. "Yes, I do have my boys. And I never stop thanking God for them. They keep me going."

The sisters had ambled some distance from the house to a weathered garden bench beneath a sprawling maple tree. Janet sat and patted the seat beside her. "Enough about me. Tell me about you."

Christa sat and crossed her long legs. "There's not much to tell. You already know I work at the City Library. Oh, and I'm engaged..."

"Oh, and by the way, I'm engaged, but it's nothing important?" Janet mocked. "Congratulations. Is it Nigel ? What's taken him so long?" Nigel Chambers was the up-and-coming insurance broker whose eye Christa had caught shortly before Janet ran off with Marty. Nigel and his financial success and wealth potential were all Christa talked about in those days.

"Nigel Chambers is ancient news. He found someone who would supply the benefits without the license."

"Then you made a lucky escape."

Christa pulled a multi-lobed leaf from a maple branch just above her shoulder. "I suppose so, but I did like his bank account." She shot a mocking glance at Janet. "You didn't do so badly in that department yourself, despite Marty's wandering."

Wandering...? That's what her sister called it? Christa had no idea, and Janet had no intention of setting her straight.

Instead, she snagged Christa's left hand to inspect her sister's engagement ring — and found the finger bare.

"Where's the ring?"

"There isn't one. I said I'd rather have a really spectacular wedding band. You know, one set with diamonds big enough to knock your eye out."

Marty had given Janet an impressive diamond solitaire. Too bad she hadn't had the presence of mind at the time to question how someone barely out of high school could afford such a pricy item. Janet wondered who was wearing the ring now...

She gave her head a shake. "So this new man, the one you're engaged to, are you sure about him, Chris?"

Christa folded the leaf in half, careful to match the lobes and make the halves exactly equal. "What's to be sure about? He's a straightforward guy with no dark secrets. He's never been married, is respected by all. Mom and Dad treat him like a son. We met at church."

"Do you love him?"

Her sister forced the leaf into yet another fold. "Janet, you and I both know that love is over-rated. Not everyone experiences the kind of love they show in chick flicks and romance novels. Maybe I'm not capable of that kind of love. All I know is, we're comfortable together," she waggled perfectly shaped eyebrows, "and we make a very impressive couple."

Janet's mouth quirked. "What does this highly respected fellow do for a living?"

"He's a banker."

For some reason the man from The Tireman flashed to Janet's mind, but she dismissed him immediately. Despite the way he'd embarrassed her, she suspected he fit into the respected-by-all category, too, but she didn't want to think about him.

"I suppose it's your fiancé who's coming for dinner tonight."

"Probably. Like I said, Mom and Dad think the world of him."

Just as it should be. Exactly opposite to how things had been with her and Marty.

"When's the wedding?"

"Early December."

Only four months away. "Would you have invited me?" Janet's tone was teasing, but at the same time, she was curious to know.

"I'm inviting you now. In fact, I want you to be my bridesmaid. Will you do it?"

"I'd be honored."

"Super." Christa gave her a one-armed hug. "I hope this isn't going to be a short visit, Janet. It would be awfully nice if you and the boys could stay for a while. I know Mom and Dad would appreciate it. And with Marty gone, there's nothing keeping you in Sacramento."

Oh, my dear sister, you have no idea how true that is...

Chapter 5

Janet quartered the potato she'd just peeled and added it to the cooking pot. She was feeling remarkably mellow. Her father's welcome had been no less warm than her mother's, for which Janet was deeply grateful and profoundly humbled. After years of next-to-no communication, they had both received her with open arms. No condemnation, no questions, no demands to know why she'd shunned them. Eventually they'd hear the whole sordid story, but not now. That was for later, when she was back on her feet and in control of her life. She'd share her immediate plans, sketchy though they were, at supper. But for now she just wanted to catch her breath, and rest and regroup in the arms of her family.

There was something deeply restorative about working in the kitchen with Christa and her mother, who was chatting about anything that came to mind, just happy to have both her girls at home and her family around her.

"Can't wait to meet Prince Charming," Janet called to Christa who was setting the dining room table.

Her sister ducked her head around the corner to consult the rooster's stomach. "He'll be here any minute. Punctuality is his middle name."

"Naturally," Janet teased. "Christa Caldwell would settle for nothing less."

She filled the cooking pot with water and set it on the burner to heat.

"Prince Charming, as you call him, just drove up,"

Verna announced, gathering garden-fresh green beans into a casserole dish and drizzling them with tomato juice, then sprinkling bacon bits over the top.

Janet pretended to preen, fluffing her hopelessly tangled curls and straightening her not-so-fresh T-shirt. "Do I look okay, Mom? I certainly wouldn't want to embarrass my big sister."

Verna chuckled. "Looks like you may have to wait a while to meet Prince Charming, as you call him. He's with Dad and the twins, who appear to be talking the man's head off. Those two have to be the friendliest little bunnies I've ever met."

Janet sighed. "A little too friendly sometimes."

Christa seemed in no hurry to acknowledge or welcome her fiancé. She continued laying out the cutlery and placing drinking glasses at each setting. 'Comfortable together' must mean 'You've been here before, buddy. Look after yourself.'

By the time the back door finally opened and the male contingent trooped inside, the potatoes were mashed, the green beans heated through, the chicken carved, and the food plated and ready for the table.

"Don't forget to wash your hands, boys," Janet called.

"Where's the bathroom?" That was Freddy.

"Follow me."

Janet froze. A tingle of awareness raised goosebumps on her arms.

She'd heard that voice before.

What were the chances that her sister's fiancé was the same man who'd maligned her sons back at The Tireman? The man in whose debt she probably was for a tankful of gas? The man whose voice sent shivers of awareness zigzagging down her spine?

What were the odds?

With her luck? About one in one.

* * *

It was obvious to Grant Brooks that Janet Caldwell O'Grady was not enjoying her welcome home dinner, and he was pretty sure he was the cause.

He wouldn't blame her if she still felt raw over the way he'd pointed out her boys' misdemeanor at The Tireman. She had a right. It was none of his business, especially since he'd had no idea of her circumstance, or even who she was, for that matter.

It was a shock when Toni informed him Janet was Christa's sister. No wonder she'd looked oddly familiar. There was something about her posture, and the shape of her face...

Being forewarned had given him a distinct advantage when Christa introduced them before dinner, but he'd given no indication to Christa or her parents that he and Janet had met before. He wanted to spare Janet embarrassing explanations. Of course, that little consideration nowhere near made amends. Nor did filling her gas tank. But it was the least he could do.

While she continued to be wary, it was interesting that her kids seemed totally unaffected by his part in the incident at The Tireman. The moment they'd seen him step out of his car, they were on him like tacks on a magnet. They were cute little fellows, full of spunk and energy. Curious, and smart. And interacting with them fed a mysterious, deeply buried yen to have children of his. Which wasn't likely to happen; Christa had made her feelings on the subject crystal clear. More than once.

For her, it was non-negotiable.

Grant shoved his disappointment back into the dark cavern where it lived and forced himself to concentrate on what was happening around the table. The atmosphere was thick enough a person could lose their way in it. He'd seen the looks Bill and Verna exchanged from time to time. They wanted a full disclosure from their youngest daughter, but they were biding their time. He wouldn't mind knowing about her, too, but this was strictly a family matter. He didn't need to be a part of it, something confirmed by the uneasy glances Janet cast his way whenever a personal question was directed at her. The last thing she wanted was to air the details of her life within his hearing.

He respected that, and after the boys had finished their dessert (Verna's homemade peach pie with French vanilla ice cream) he turned to the twins. "Well, fellows, how about we men excuse ourselves and go outside and play?"

Freddy's brown eyes grew saucer-sized. "Really? Oh, boy! Can we, Mommy?"

"Please?" Teddy added his voice to the plea.

Janet hesitated. The look she angled at Grant spoke of distrust and displeasure. Was she reluctant to put her boys in the care of someone who had insinuated they were junior delinquents? Come on, he wanted to protest, that was supposed to have been a little joke. No harm intended.

Or, he wondered, was her hesitation prompted by the fear he'd read in her posture when she'd huddled over her young out there by the roadside?

"Please, Mommy?" This was Freddy.

Grant hadn't known eyes could dance and plead at

the same time.

"Well—" Janet pressed her lips together, and a pair of dimples appeared in her cheeks. He was momentarily distracted from the business at hand and was grateful for Teddy's timely intervention.

The boy leaned close to his mother and informed her in a voice that was supposed to be a whisper but was clearly audible to all, "Grandpa knows a lot about bugs and birds, Mommy, but he's no good at running-around games. And you know, me and Freddy love running-around games. A lot."

Even Bill stifled a chuckle behind his hand.

Janet sighed. "Well, okay... I guess it's all right."

"Oh, boy!" The twins were out of their chairs in a flash. "Thanks for dinner, Grandma. Can we play football?" The rapid-fire words were aimed simultaneously at their grandmother and at Grant, who had shucked his suit jacket and was stripping off his silk tie in preparation.

"We'd need a football."

"Teddy and me have one in the car." Freddy tugged at Janet's arm. "Can you get it for us, Mommy? Please?"

"The--uh--the car's unlocked..."

Grant glanced at Janet. The fact that her eyes appeared stuck on his fingers loosening the top two buttons of his white dress shirt created an odd sensation his throat that made it difficult to speak. "I'll take good care of them," he managed.

She blinked at the sound of his voice. Looked up, then away. Color stained her cheeks.

"Hurry, Mr. Grant." The twins were literally bouncing with anticipation, which was probably a good thing because it effectively shattered whatever weird and disconcerting thing was going on between him and their mother.

Grant fixed his attention on the twins. "Under the circumstances," he said, "you boys may as well call me Uncle Grant."

"What are circastancers?" Teddy, apparently, was the 'word' man.

Grant chuckled and ruffled the boy's hair.

"It means the way things are," Grant told him.

Teddy looked up with admiration in his eyes. "Oh, like the circastancers is we're going out to play football?"

"You've got it exactly right."

* * *

The sound of high fives carried from the back porch to the four still seated around the dining table. Janet was the only one not wearing a smile.

Truth be told, she wanted to cry, and she had Grant Brooks to thank for that. The tender way he'd cupped her little son's head with his hand almost undid her. Neither of her boys had ever experienced that sort of affection from a man before. Certainly not from Marty. To their father, the children were a noisy nuisance.

But why, oh why, did love and affection have to come from this particular man? Her boys were like Play-Doh in his hands, and given the 'circastancers,' she feared it could mean devastation for all of them down the road.

Janet heaved a lung-deep sigh.

When she turned back to the table, she found her parents and her sister watching her, their smiles diluted by half. She had no doubt they were waiting to hear her explanation of why, suddenly and with no advance warning, she'd made the trek home.

Problem was, she didn't know how much to tell them. It would hardly be fair to burden her parents with her worries and woes, especially her father. So she would probably keep the truth to herself and handle things on her own.

Just as she'd been doing for the past eight years.

In the end, she simply said, "The boys and I are moving back to Ever Green."

The half-smiles bled away completely.

"There's nothing to keep us in Sacramento now that Marty's gone, and I thought it would be good for the boys to be near all of you. I was hoping we could stay with you until I can find a job and a place for the three of us to live."

Janet saw the look that passed between her parents, and her heart took a sickening nosedive. They didn't want her here.

"Of course you're welcome to stay with us, dear," her mother said, "but you have to remember, our house isn't nearly as big as what you're used to. And with your dad not well..."

Her father interrupted. "Don't you worry about me, but I'm afraid you're going to have trouble finding work, honey. The economy's pretty flat in this part of the state right now. Jobs are scarce."

"I'm willing to do anything." Janet divided a quick glance between her mother and father. "In fact, I was thinking maybe I could work for you on the farm."

Another exchange of looks. "We already have a couple working for us, Janet," her mother said. "Juan and Maria Rodriguez."

"I know, but you could let them go and save the

money. I'll work for nothing."

Verna's eyes were soft with regret. "They really need the money."

Not as much as I do, Mom...

She blew out a noisy breath. "Okay, that's out. Is your library looking for anyone, Chris?"

Christa shook her head. "'Fraid not."

"Then I'll start searching first thing in the morning." She'd ration the gas in her tank, make it last as long as possible. "Hotels are always looking for cleaning staff."

It wasn't like she had any marketable skills or career training. As everyone around the table was well aware, she'd run away the week after graduation to marry Marty O'Grady who'd promised her the moon. When it came to money, he'd delivered in spades. But what the others didn't know was that the moon had very quickly proven to be made of dirty, smelly cheese.

"I'll find something." She forced a cheery note into her voice. "Come on Christa, let's clean things up. Mom, you go relax with Dad."

A full moon shot arrows of silvery light through the partially closed window blinds and onto the faces of the twins who were fast asleep in their 'camp bed' which took up most of the floor space in Janet's girlhood bedroom.

Convincing Freddy and Teddy to camp out on the floor took no persuasion at all. She'd hauled the duvets and pillows in from the Jeep to make a cozy bed for them and they'd fallen asleep immediately. This was all one big adventure for them, and that's exactly how Janet wanted to keep it.

The boys had played outside with Grant for more than an hour. As she and Christa cleaned up the kitchen, Janet had caught glimpses of the three of them through the kitchen window. At one point, Grant had a boy tucked under each arm and was deking his way past imaginary defenders to an arbitrary goal line where they all collapsed in a heap on the grass and congratulated each another on the make-believe touchdown.

She couldn't ever remember Marty playing like that with his sons. Marty had never interacted with the boys. His indifference had bordered on abuse, but she shouldn't have been surprised. He'd warned her from the beginning that he didn't want children. Once she'd become pregnant with the twins, he had no further interest in her, either.

But that was ancient history.

Her present history was right here, right now, in this room.

Her mother was right. The room was much smaller than she remembered, Janet decided as she surveyed it from the single bed she hadn't occupied for close to a decade. It probably seemed small because she was accustomed to the enormous master suite in the Sacramento house.

Marty hadn't shared the suite. On the rare occasion he was home for the night, he used a bedroom off his office where, it turned out, he'd conducted other questionable activities, as well. The extent of those activities was still to be determined, but the apparent fruits of his labor were hidden in her leather bag which was now stashed in a far corner of the closet at the foot of her bed. While looking for a secure place to hide it, she'd come across a worn blue denim shoulder bag from decades past that would carry what she needed until she figured out what to do with the incriminating evidence in the leather purse.

The contents of the papers had shocked her and raised a myriad questions she couldn't begin to answer. She recognized immediately that the information in the papers was incriminating and dangerous. Dangerous enough that the lives of her precious twin boys were at risk. It was discovering the papers that had prompted her to pack the boys into the Jeep in the middle of the night and leave Sacramento far behind.

She knew the evidence couldn't stay hidden forever. In the very near future she'd have to figure out what to do with it. But now wasn't the time.

She was home, and her boys were safe.

That's all that mattered.

For the moment.

Chapter 6

As usual, the twins awoke eager to get on with things. And though she could count her own hours of sleep on one hand without using all her fingers, Janet knew she had no choice but to get up with them and do her best to minimize the commotion they were bound to make. She settled them in the living room to watch a TV show about scorpions with the volume turned low.

Then she headed to the kitchen to make coffee.

The scent of dew-dampened earth wafted through the open kitchen window and the early morning sun was refracting off a million diamond dewdrops on the closely-clipped lawn. It might have been soothing and comforting to the senses had it not been for the urgency nipping at her nerves.

She had just added grounds to the coffee maker basket when Christa appeared in the kitchen wearing silky navy pajamas that still managed to look elegant.

They greeted each other in low tones.

Janet nodded in the general direction of their parents' bedroom. "Is this usual? Mom and Dad sleeping this late?" Through all her years at home, they'd always risen before the sun.

Christa pulled a mug from the cupboard and watched the coffee drip into the glass pot. "Dad needs his sleep these days, and Mom likes to wait until he's awake before she gets up. He had a lot of excitement yesterday."

She didn't have to add that having extra people

around, especially energetic little people, had increased the strain on the household.

Janet knew the truth of it.

She needed to find a job and alternate living arrangements. Fast.

"Do Mom and Dad still get the *Olympian*?"

The coffee was finally ready and Christa poured herself a cup and savored a careful sip. "It'll be in the mailbox. Dad usually takes a stroll to the end of the lane to get it."

"The boys and I will do it this morning."

"But it's Dad's morning exercise. What's the hurry?"

"I need to look for a job, Christa. And there's school for the boys to think about. There are less than ten days before school starts and I want to get them enrolled." Her heart sank just a bit thinking about it, because driving to the school would mean burning precious fuel that she'd hoped to conserve as long as possible. Still, it couldn't be helped.

Christa split a multi-grain bagel and slid the halves into the toaster. She leaned against the counter and continued to drink her coffee while the bagel toasted. "I don't mean to meddle in your business, Janet, but I mentioned your situation to Grant last night..."

Thanks a lot, Sis. Just what I needed...

"I don't know if this interests you or not, but Grant owns a house that no one's living in. It belonged to Pop Smith, his grandfather, who passed away in March. Grant hasn't had time to do anything with the house. He said if you're willing to clean it up and get it ready for sale, you and the boys can live in it rent-free until it sells." Christa rescued the bagel halves from the toaster and spread them with a thin layer of low-fat cream cheese. "I must warn you, though, cleaning that house wouldn't be a simple matter of vacuuming and dusting. Pop was a serious hoarder. It would be a lot of work."

Janet mulled over the unexpected offer while she prepared a breakfast of Shreddies and peanut buttered toast for herself and the boys.

"Where is this house?"

"About a half mile east of The Tireman."

Relatively close to Ever Green Acres. Janet might be anxious to be out of her parents' hair, but she still liked the idea of her children being close to their grandparents. There was a certain wholesomeness about that. Not to mention security...

"Like I say, it would be a lot of work."

She'd been prepared to do far more strenuous work than cleaning a house. And having no expenses would be a godsend. Surely, once the boys were in school, she could get a part-time job of some sort to put food on the table. In the meantime, she knew, Ever Green Acres would supply all the fresh produce they could want.

It just might work.

However, something deep inside nagged at her sense of propriety. In the dark hours of night she'd thought a lot about Grant Brooks and the traitorous way her body and her senses behaved when he was around. It was inexplicable and frankly disturbing. Definitely unwanted. And under the circumstances, something she needed to get under control. Because Grant was going to marry her sister, and there was no excuse whatsoever for her to have any sort of intimate feelings about him.

Avoidance, she'd decided, was the best strategy, but the arrangement Christa was proposing didn't exactly allow for avoidance, did it.

On the other hand, did she have a choice?

Besides, hadn't Christa just told her Grant hadn't done anything with the house in five months? That had to mean he spent minimal time there, right? And knowing someone was living in the house would give him even less reason to come around.

Right?

She sincerely hoped so.

Christa gave a bite of bagel a thorough chewing before sliding Janet an inscrutable look. "Grant couldn't stop talking about your boys."

Janet looked around in surprise. "Really?"

"Grant loves kids."

"Well, the twins certainly enjoyed his attention." Janet placed three cereal bowls on the table and removed a trio of spoons from the cutlery drawer with a minimum of clatter. "He seems very good with children."

"It's one of the things we don't agree on." The way Christa wrapped her arm around her waist was almost self-protective.

"How do you mean?"

"He wants children when we're married and I don't."

Janet wasn't sure how to respond. No doubt her sister had her reasons for not wanting a family, but it would be a shame, because it was obvious Grant would make a great father. It seemed a sin, almost, to rob him of the privilege.

"You know," she said gently, "a lot of women feel the way you do until they actually have children of their own. I'd never have pegged myself as mommy material, but now I don't know how I'd live without my boys."

She gave her sister a reassuring smile. "You'll work it out."

Christa's pursed lips communicated her doubt before she turned away to dust her hands over the sink. "So what do I tell Grant?"

"About having children? Don't you think that's between the two of you?"

"No, silly. What do I tell him about Pop's house?"

Janet smothered a burst of laughter. "The house..." Her amusement disappeared. "What do you think about it, Chris?"

"I think it's a perfect solution." Christa shrugged. "I can't see myself cleaning it, but if I were in your shoes and didn't mind the work, I'd grab it."

"So you have no objections to me living in your fiancé's house?"

Christa stared. "It's not like Grant lives there."

Janet placed the Shreddies box on the table and planted her hands on her hips. "Okay, then, I'll do it." She ignored the misgivings pecking at the back of her mind. "Please thank Grant, and tell him that, yes, I'm definitely interested."

She spent the rest of the day wondering what on earth she'd just done.

* * *

Grant felt a surge of anticipation as he turned the Lexus into the lane of the Caldwell farm on Saturday morning. Given the cool reception Janet had given him at dinner two nights before, he was surprised when she agreed to let him drive her and the boys to Pop's house.

His anticipation probably had to do with the twins, he told himself. As he showered that morning, he'd found himself thinking about Freddy and Teddy, and grinning like a clown. They were so enthusiastic, so responsive to the tiniest bit of affection. Just remembering made him smile all over again.

The smile widened when the door of the farmhouse flew open and the boys burst through shouting, "He's here, Mommy! Uncle Grant is here!"

Grant stopped the Lexus beside Janet's Jeep and got out.

"Whoa, cowboys," he exclaimed when Freddy and Teddy barreled into him and wrapped their arms around his waist. The adoration in their eyes brought an uncharacteristic lump to his throat. He ruffled their hair with his hands.

He looked up at the sound of the screen door slapping shut to see Janet starting down the walk. She looked winsome and wholly unpretentious in a short-sleeved white t-shirt and a casual, white denim skirt that showed off her long legs. The combination made Grant's mouth go a little dry.

Her cocoa-brown curls were more disciplined today, he noticed. She'd swept them back and fastened them at the back of her head somehow so they tumbled to her shoulders like a glossy chocolate waterfall.

Grant had to clear his throat before he could speak. "'Morning."

"Good morning."

She was looking at him in a way that had him hoping he'd paid sufficient attention to his own preparations this morning. He probably should have shaved, and maybe done more than scrub his hair dry with the bath towel. He hadn't really been thinking when he threw on a black polo shirt and cargo shorts and shoved his feet into his favorite Birkenstocks.

It was almost a relief when Janet glanced down and fumbled in her blue shoulder bag for her car keys. "The boys need their booster chairs," she said, sounding a little breathless. "They're in the Jeep."

Attending to the transfer was a welcome diversion. This shouldn't be happening, he told himself as he extracted the seats from her vehicle and transferred them to the Lexus. Janet was his fiancée's sister, for pete's sake. He shouldn't be noticing what she was wearing, or how nice she looked, or feeling insecure about his own appearance.

Get a grip, man...

He flashed a grin at the boys. "All set, men?"

"Yup!" they chorused, and scrambled in. Grant secured their seatbelts, and gave each one a little fist bump on the shoulder.

Freddy and Teddy giggled in response.

Grant looked across at Janet. "You ready?"

She nodded and slid into the passenger seat of the SUV.

Grant swung in behind the wheel and started the engine. "It's a beautiful day. Do you mind having the windows down?"

Janet shook her head. "Not at all."

It *was* a beautiful day. It was only nine o'clock, but the August sunshine had already warmed the morning air. Above the jagged tree line, the sky was clear and cloudless, a pale cerulean blue that carried the promise of a perfect West Coast day.

More arresting for Grant than the view outside was the subtle fragrance filling the interior of his vehicle. Even with the windows open, he could smell vanilla. It had to be Janet's perfume. Or maybe her shampoo. He had the inexplicable urge to lean closer and inhale deeply, or maybe smooth one of those cocoa curls between his fingers to see if the scent rubbed off...

He squelched the thought and shoved the Lexus into gear. As they started down the lane, he once again focused his attention to the twins in the backseat.

"What's new with you, boys?"

Freddy leaned into his seatbelt. "We're going to First Grade soon."

"In ten days." His twin held up both hands, all fingers splayed.

Grant grinned. "You happy about that?"

"Yeah," they chorused.

He cast a glance Janet's way. "You've already enrolled them?" Christa had told him Janet was looking for a temporary place to live, but she obviously planned to stay a while if the boys were going to school.

"I took them to tour the school yesterday and meet their teacher. They're pretty jazzed, especially with the prospect of riding the school bus."

"Ever Green Elementary?"

Janet nodded. "The same one I attended when I was a kid. What about you?" She darted a look at him.

"We lived in Olympia, but we came out here a lot. I remember begging my mom to let me live with Pop and Gram so I could attend Ever Green Elementary instead of the city school. I think I had the idea there wouldn't be as much work here. In any case, my mother didn't fall for the plan."

They exchanged an easy smile, which had the effect of increasing Grant's heart rate.

It only took a few minutes to reach Pop Smith's

house. Grant experienced a wave of chagrin and regret as the wood and stone, two story came into view. With its gabled windows on the upper level, its graceful sweeping roof and pillared porch wrapping around two sides, it was a striking edifice. But even from the bottom of the driveway, neglect was clearly evident. Leaves and twigs littered the roof and porch. The wide brickwork steps that gave access to the front walk were seriously narrowed by an accumulation of moss and rotting debris. On either side of the steps were S-shaped planters that had once showcased Gram's precious roses. Now they were little more than an untidy tangle of growth. And as for the lawn... Well, it looked more like a hay meadow.

He should have been out here long ago looking after the place.

"This was your grandparents' home?"

"'Fraid so." Grant couldn't keep a note of sadness from his voice. "Pop carried on here after Gram died, but not very well. He did the best he could, but he just didn't have the heart to look after things the way Gram liked. He passed away this spring." Grant sent Janet an apologetic look. "The place is mine now, but I confess I haven't looked after it any better than Pop did." A muscle twitched in his jaw as he surveyed the yard. "Gram would weep if she could see this. She always made sure the place looked like a park."

The twins saw absolutely nothing wrong with the grassy space. "Wow!" Freddy exclaimed. "Can we run around?"

"All right," Janet said once she'd confirmed Grant had no objections. "But stay close."

While the twins blazed trails through the grass that

was knee-high in places, Janet followed Grant to the back of the house where he fitted a key in the door lock. He hesitated before opening it.

"I should warn you, Pop was a bit of a packrat. That's one of the reasons I haven't done anything with the place. Once you see the inside, you may decide you aren't interested, either. If that's the case, I'll understand completely."

Chapter 7

Janet appreciated Grant's warning, but at this point, the place would pretty much have to be condemned for her to turn it down. One step through the back door, however, lent credence to his statement.

Janet found herself in a mudroom so crammed with rubbish that only the narrowest passage remained to walk through. Stacks of newspapers and magazines, some higher than her own five-foot-six-inch height, looked ready to topple at any moment. Wall pegs meant for one coat each held many more. Bulging cardboard boxes piled several high filled all the available wall space, and only the fronts of a white enamel washer/dryer set were visible. The tops were totally obscured by heaps of plastic bags spewing what Janet could only surmise was trash.

The kitchen was little better. Canned goods and boxed grocery items obscured the counter tops. Only their expiry dates would give a clue to how long they'd been there. And surely the stacks of empty plastic tubs represented every margarine, sour cream, and yogurt purchase Grant's Pop and Gram had ever made. A life's worth of plastic grocery bags burst from cupboard doors. And what could possibly be inside the cardboard boxes stacked floor-to-ceiling along the walls?

Grant shook his head as he opened, then quickly closed the door to the walk-in pantry. "I'm sorry about all this," he said, "but I did warn you."

She was spared comment by the sound of the twins

at the back door.

"In here." She threaded her way back through the mudroom to let them in.

The two stepped inside and looked around, their eyes wide with wonder.

"Wow!" Freddy exclaimed. "What a mess!"

"Yeah, what a mess!" Teddy echoed. Then, "But you know what's good about this, Freddy?"

"What?"

"We didn't make it!"

And they departed as quickly as they'd arrived.

Grant grinned, then quirked a doubtful eyebrow at her. "Are you game to see the rest?"

She shrugged. "Lead on."

The living room was impossibly cluttered. Horizontal blinds on the windows were shut tight, possibly to prevent the upholstered furniture pieces from fading, though that would be difficult since virtually none of the surfaces were exposed. The lack of light turned the room into a murky dungeon, but Janet was able to identify piles of discarded blankets and clothing on sofas and chairs, and stacks of dusty books and magazines scattered everywhere. An area rug whose navy and cream pattern was scarcely discernible covered the hardwood floor in front of a soot-stained brick fireplace, and in the ceiling-to-floor bookcases on either side of it, a messy jumble of hardcover and paperback books leaned every which way.

The house had three bedrooms, the furnishings of which were covered with more dust than Janet supposed she had ever seen before. Dust motes released from the carpets by their feet rode what shafts of sunlight were able to sneak through the grimy window blinds. Closets spilled a cargo of clothes through doors that probably hadn't shut in years.

And they'd only toured the upper levels of the house...

Grant led her down to the basement where the concrete walls were lined with row upon row of shelving. One section held nothing but empty glass jars in every imaginable size.

"Gram was famous for her canning and preserves," he explained when Janet remarked on the quantity of glassware.

Other shelves bore even more canned goods. Janet spied a row of oversized storage bins. Hand-printed labels identified the contents as staples like flour, sugar and the like.

Grant spread his hands, palms up. "What can I say? Pop and Gram had a Depression mentality. They learned it from their parents who hailed from the Mid-West and believed the next Great Depression was just around the corner."

To this point, Janet had absorbed it all with little comment. "What do you want done with the food?" she asked as they made their way back to the kitchen.

Grant shook his head helplessly. "I don't know. Use whatever you can yourself, I guess, and we'll donate the rest of it to some soup kitchen or food bank. The easiest thing would be to bring in a giant disposal bin and chuck everything, but Gram and Pop were big on recycling and caring for the Earth. I know it would make a whole lot more work for you, but I'd like to honor their wish as much as possible."

"I've no problem with that." Janet was an advocate of recycling herself. Besides, the longer it took to get the work done, the longer she and the boys would have a place to stay. Long enough, she hoped, for her to figure out a satisfactory future course of action.

"Does this mean you're willing to take on the job?" Grant was regarding her with a mix of amazement, doubt and admiration. "I thought you'd take one look and run."

She'd already gone that route and look where it landed her.

"Do you care when we move in?"

"Anytime is fine with me." Grant dug in his pocket for the key and placed it in her hand.

Janet closed her fingers around it. Still warm from his body heat, the key represented more to her than Grant could ever know. Not only was it a symbol of safety and an answer to where she and her boys could hide away, but Janet viewed it as a critical element in putting her life back together.

It felt good in her hand.

It felt like hope.

"Is this afternoon too soon?"

"Whenever." Grant's hand reached out to clasp her upper arm. His eyes were warm. "Look, Janet... I really appreciate that you're willing to take this on," he said. "This place has always been special to me. I'm just glad that Pop's house will be lived in again."

Look away, idiot woman. Look away...

But she couldn't. The look in his eyes held her hostage and sent a wash of heat up her neck—

Until the muted ring of her cell phone deep within her shoulder bag brought her to her senses.

* * *

Grant's hand fell away from Janet's upper arm as he straightened, but the feel of her satiny skin lingered.

He cleared his throat. "You take your call. I'll see what the boys are doing."

He headed for the door, grateful for the interruption. He needed to put some distance between himself and Janet O'Grady so he could get a handle on his thoughts. They were way more personal than he figured they should be about a woman who would soon become his sister-in-law.

But how could he not admire her? Janet was the gutsiest, most courageous woman he'd ever met. Outside of his mother, that is. And when it came right down to it, there were strong similarities between the two. Both women had accepted widowhood with equanimity, it seemed, and willingly sacrificed their own interests for the good of their children.

He'd only known Janet a few days, but he already knew that her boys came first with her. And how could a person not admire that?

He wondered if Janet's family realized how dire her situation was. He'd tried to quiz Christa subtly, but his fiancée was of the opinion that Janet had no financial worries. Her husband had been successful in business and they'd lived in a mansion of a house in Sacramento, the sale of which would keep her younger sister living in luxury for years.

Grant hadn't mentioned the dollar-and-a-half worth of gas at The Tireman. That was Janet's business. But surely, if what Christa believed about her sister was true, Janet should have been able to flash any one of a deck of credit cards to pay for a full tank. She hadn't. And he'd seen her dread, her fear.

No, he was willing to bet money that Janet's family had no idea... And the fact that she was willing to plant herself in the midst of Pop's squalor said she didn't want them to know. That realization shot his protective instincts higher than they'd ever been before.

The boys were in the backyard taking turns swinging from a length of old rope that hung from the branch of a gnarled oak. The rope was all that remained of the swing Pop had rigged for him when he was a kid.

They spotted him and waved. "Hi, Uncle Grant..."

He gave his own wave and walked toward them, stopping at the foot of the oak tree. It was still healthy, he could tell, and the branch holding the rope looked sturdy enough. He gave the rope a hefty tug. No deterioration there, either.

"My granddad put up this swing for me when I was your age," he told the boys.

Freddy frowned. "This was a swing? No wonder it's broken if it's that old."

Grant gave the rope another tug. "It's not broken. But the board is missing. Wanna help me look for it?"

The boys trailed behind him to the garden shed nearby where Pop stored his lawn mower and yard tools. The door was locked, but Grant knew where to find the key. He retrieved it from the backside of a birdhouse hanging from the soffit and unlocked the door.

A wave of nostalgia smacked him hard as he stepped inside the dusty interior. Every last item reminded him of Pop, and in that moment, the pain of losing his grandfather was as keen as an open wound.

But he was given little time to grieve.

"Do you see it?" Teddy's expression, as he scanned

the shed's clutter, said he doubted that was possible.

The kid had a point. The shed was no tidier than Pop's dwelling. If Janet was game enough to take on cleaning up the house, the least he could do was deal with the garden shed. A wry smile formed at the thought.

'Game' seemed like such a weak descriptor for the twins' mother. What other woman did he know who would accept—without complaint or hesitation, mind you—the monumental task of dealing with Pop's disaster of a house? Certainly not her sister...

But he wasn't going to go there. Christa was a good woman. She just...wasn't...Janet.

Focus on the swing board, Brooks...

It didn't take long for Grant to spot the board hanging from a spike in the wall. "There it is." He cleared a path through the clutter to reach it.

The board was thick, and about ten inches wide and two feet long, with a narrow hole through the center for the rope. The twins gave it a skeptical look.

"Are you sure that's for a swing?" Freddy inquired, his eyes narrowing. "It doesn't look right to me."

"Me, either," Teddy declared. "Are you sure you know about swings?"

Grant bit down on a grin. "Hey, you two hoodlums, give me a break. Of course I know about swings. Just wait and see."

The two followed him back to the oak tree and watched with increasing impatience while he struggled to untie the decades-old knot at the rope's end. They had plenty of suggestions on how to speed up the process, some that had him choking back laughter.

What a delight these kids were! Janet was doing a

marvelous job with them. He looked forward to the fun times he'd have with them in the future. Warmth bloomed in his chest at the thought.

By the time Grant had the knot undone and a new one fixed beneath the swing board, the twins had grasped the concept of how the swing worked and were literally bouncing with anticipation. Grant gave the board and rope one last test for stability, then helped the riders aboard.

"Hang on to the rope," he warned, and gave the swing a push.

Shouts of laughter filled the yard as Freddy and Teddy swung and spun and explored the possibilities and limits of the new toy. The sounds elicited a pang that constricted Grant's chest.

Pop would have loved these kids. He'd have loved talking with them, and watching them play, and hearing their joyful laughter fill his yard. He'd have loved seeing them be happy, carefree children.

Again, the fact that they were happy and carefree and normal was a tribute to Janet.

Pop would have loved Janet, too. He'd never told Grant so, but he knew his grandfather had never really warmed to Christa, and had never fully accepted her as Grant's fiancée. Grant knew why; Pop knew Christa wasn't marrying Grant for love. It was the security and stability that marriage to him would provide that she loved. The fact that he was the sole heir to the family's banking assets didn't hurt either.

Grant wasn't stupid. He'd known from the very beginning of their relationship that a union between himself and Christa would not be based on love, at least not the kind that Pop and Gram shared. Love like that came along only for the very few. But he was fine with comfortable and convenient.

At least, he had been until recently.

He'd figured that friendship, and mutual respect, and shared Christian values would be enough for him in marriage. Now, he doubted that was true.

A sense of sadness overwhelmed him as he watched Janet's boys twist and turn and ride the old rope swing like a bucking bronco. Friendship and mutual respect were no longer enough for him, but breaking his engagement to Christa was not an option. He'd made a commitment to her, and he was a man of honor.

He would stand by that commitment.

* * *

Janet wished there was somewhere in Pop's house to sit down. She was feeling more than a little ill. Dread and uncertainty had her head spinning, and her stomach was making serious threats to purge itself. She sagged against the living room wall and waited for the feeling to pass.

Grant needn't have left when her phone rang. She hadn't answered it. According to the screen, the call was from Bart O'Grady, her late husband's twin brother and business partner.

Bart was the last person on earth she wanted to speak to.

She'd turned off the phone, reburied it in her bag, and done her best to tamp down the fear his name generated. Did he somehow know where she was? She'd heard that cell phone calls could be traced, but surely that only applied when the person answered the phone. And did Bart have the capability to do that anyway?

It probably depended on how desperate he was, and she already knew the answer to that.

Bart was six-point-one million dollars' worth of desperate.

Why he was calling was no mystery. He was after the same information he'd been demanding ever since Marty died. Initially, it was information she couldn't give, information she'd only discovered mere hours before her dead-of-the-night escape to Ever Green.

Janet felt for the house key in the pocket of her white denim skirt and wrapped her fingers around it tightly. The fact that Pop's house was off the beaten path was an added blessing for her. And even the unbelievable clutter seemed to increase the obscurity she craved, as if it would hem her and the boys in and hide them.

She closed her eyes and fought to regain normal breathing. Seeing Bart's name on her phone had constricted her lungs so badly her breath came in shallow gasps because it brought to mind his blood-chilling threats about what he'd do to her boys if she wasn't forthcoming with the information he demanded. She wasn't fooled. That information was so important to Bart he would never stop looking for her. There was too much at stake for him not to search until he found her and got the incriminating evidence she'd sewn into the lining of her leather bag which was currently hidden in a dark corner of her parents' home.

Janet's smile held no humor. Fortunately, there would be no problem finding a safe hiding place for it in this house.

Of course, she couldn't sit on the evidence forever, and she also knew that the longer she put Bart off, the more dangerous he would become and the greater the likelihood he would make good on his threats. The problem was, she didn't know what to do with her discovery. Nor did she know who to trust with it. She needed time to figure it all out.

Janet pushed away from the wall and attempted to shift her focus to her surroundings. Now that she was away from Grant's unsettling presence, she was able to give the space a more thorough study. The room exhibited some exquisite woodwork, especially around the fireplace and the bookshelves. What she could see of the floors looked like quality hardwood. And could that soiled area rug possibly be Aubusson? Her breath quickened as she imagined the space minus the detritus, scrubbed clean, surfaces gleaming and smelling of lemon oil. It really was a lovely old house. She could hardly wait to begin restoring it to its former glory.

One of her first orders of business would be cleaning the big kitchen window that looked out on the yard, because despite its unkempt condition, the yard was quite lovely. A pair of peach trees on the far right were studded with golden fruit, and a thick-trunked oak shaded much of the yard with its gnarly branches.

The oak tree held a swing, and Grant was out there right now watching the boys play on it. Even through the closed window, Janet could hear their shouts of laughter. She'd heard it said that children could instinctively judge a person's character. If that were true, it was obvious her boys deemed Grant Brooks to be thoroughly trustworthy.

Did she believe that about him?

Perhaps, if she ignored the episode at The Tireman. Although, to his credit, Grant hadn't embarrassed her by recounting the incident later at her parents' house. And today, he'd been nothing but friendly and totally respectful toward her——a rare quality these days. At least in the men she'd known.

But there was the disconcerting matter of how he made her feel. How his voice set every cell in her body on high alert. How looking at him made her knees a little weak. And how the loving way he handled her boys turned her to total mush.

Or, was she so pathetic and needy that she was falling under the spell of the first man to treat her with decency?

Janet shook her head. Whatever was happening, she'd have to deal with it. Grant Brooks was engaged to her sister and was beyond off limits to her, but the arrangement he was offering at Pop's house was too good to pass up.

They camped again that night. Janet tucked her boys into the bed she arranged on the floor of the least cluttered bedroom. She'd vacuumed the floor space thoroughly and opened the window to let in the fresh evergreen-scented air. Every blanket and duvet they'd brought from Sacramento comprised their mattress, and even Janet had to admit, it was like sleeping on a feather bed.

Stars twinkled in the black sky beyond the open window and the soothing sounds of night floated on a gentle evening breeze. Night birds cooed their soft lullabies.

Janet settled into the camp bed between her boys, feeling more content than she'd dared to let herself be in a long time. Danger still lurked, and she was still penniless, but for this one moment in time, she was at peace.

Freddy and Teddy lay with their hands behind their heads.

"I like Uncle Grant," Freddy declared, his voice growing husky with sleep.

Teddy spoke through a cavernous yawn. "Me, too. Mommy, do you like Uncle Grant?"

Fortunately, it became a rhetorical question as sleep captured both boys.

A rhetorical, but troubling question. Did she like Grant Brooks? Yes, she had to admit, she did like him. More than she had a right to, more than she wanted to. Because Grant belonged to her sister. And given the feelings she'd just acknowledged, her only hope for self-preservation was to keep an extra-close guard on her heart, and as much as possible, staying out of Grant's way.

She had no other choice.

Chapter 8

"**Mommy**, your phone is ringing."

Teddy was calling from the upstairs bedroom where he and Freddy were supposed to be getting dressed.

"Mommy — ?"

"See who it is." Janet carried the cereal bowls they'd used for breakfast to the sink. The boxed cereal had tasted stale, and they'd had to eat it with diluted canned milk she'd found in the pantry. The boys weren't keen on the taste, but she'd sprinkled on some brown sugar and added chopped peaches from the tree outside. At least their stomachs were full.

"The long part starts with C."

Caldwell — ? Her mother, no doubt, checking to see if they'd survived their first night in Pop Smith's house. "It's probably Grandma. You can answer it."

"How do I answer?"

"Press the green button and say hello."

A minute later, Teddy pounded down the stairs, one sock on, one sock off. "Grandma says they'll pick us up for church in one hour." He repeated the "one hour" and extended his forefinger to make sure the message was clear and received.

Church? She hadn't planned on going to church this morning, but she really should. How could she expect God to answer her prayers if she wasn't willing to meet with Him in worship? Besides, her boys needed to be in church.

Janet hadn't paid attention to God in a lot of years.

Not regularly, at least. Marty wanted nothing to do with church or religion, and in order to keep the tenuous peace, she hadn't attend services, either. But she'd told her boys about God and His Son Jesus, and taught them to pray. Sometimes she envied their simple, uncomplicated faith.

It had taken Marty's death and the reality of how hopeless her situation was to force her back to God. She'd called out to Him. Begged for help. Pleaded for direction. Asked for a clear answer to her dilemma. She'd tried to wait patiently for His answer, but then Bart entered the picture and the situation became dangerous. Instead of waiting for Divine direction, she'd bundled up the boys in the middle of the night and sped away to the only place that seemed safe to her — Ever Green.

Well, if they were going to church, she'd definitely have to speak to Freddy and Teddy about being quiet during the service. It would be a stretch. Maybe they could find a seat near the back.

As it turned out, persuading her boys to sit quietly wasn't the only challenge. The five of them had scarcely stepped inside the sanctuary before the twins' bat radar spotted Grant sitting with Christa in a pew halfway to the front. Freddy gave Janet's arm a tug. "Can we sit with Uncle Grant? Please?"

Sitting anywhere near Grant Brooks was the last thing Janet wanted to do. It was exactly opposite to her vow to self the night before to avoid him. The effect he had on her was hard to explain and made no sense at all.

Why hadn't it occurred to her when she agreed to go to church that he and Christa would be there? Christa had told her the two had met in church.

She looked longingly at the vacant back pew, but her mother had other ideas. Verna patted Freddy on the head. "Of course we can sit with Uncle Grant," she said. "We always do."

Her mother led the way. Both Grant and Christa greeted the boys with a smile and Christa obligingly slid over so both twins could claim space beside Grant.

Janet's mother gave her a nudge. "You sit next to Freddy."

That would put her way too close to Grant for comfort, but short of making a scene right there in the aisle, Janet had no choice but to move in until a mere six-year-old's body separated them.

She mumbled a quick greeting to Grant and Christa, then fixed her eyes firmly on the front of the sanctuary.

In every way that counted, she felt out of place. Her brief glance at Grant and Christa showed Grant looking stunning in his tailored suit and tie, and her sister gorgeous in a turquoise two-piece that accentuated her magnificent aquamarine eyes and no doubt showed off her perfect, willowy figure. Dressed as she was in her white denim skirt and a plain salmon-colored T-shirt, Janet felt dowdy by comparison. She'd gathered her hair into a quick twist and secured the careless knot at the top of her head with a couple of bamboo chopsticks she'd found in a kitchen drawer. How tacky was that?

But her appearance wasn't the only thing that made Janet feel conspicuous. The journey up the aisle had revealed a number of familiar faces from years gone by, people who no doubt remembered her as "that rebellious Caldwell girl." She could imagine the behind-hand whispers. *"That's got to be Janet. You know, the one who ran away with that O'Grady boy? He was a bad one...*

Tsk, tsk. What a heartache for her parents. It's no wonder her father is ill. What's she doing back here, I wonder?"

Somehow Janet made it through the service, which went by largely as a blur. She was amazed at how quiet her boys were. They even declined the opportunity to go to Children's Church and opted to stay pressed close to Grant's side like appendages to his body.

Seeing them like that brought a salty wetness to her eyes. They'd only known the man for a few days, but already they appeared to view him as a father figure. Fortunately, Grant didn't seem to mind, but Janet could see all manner of complications on the road ahead.

God – ? If You're there, You'll have to show me how to handle this...

At the end of the service, Janet quickly slipped to the aisle to give Grant and Christa plenty of space to exit the pew. She avoided Grant's eyes when he smiled at her, frustrated at the color she knew was seeping into her face. What was she? Some high school girl with a crush on the cute boy in class.

Verna gave Grant's shoulder an affectionate pat. "These two are off now to a fancy charity do in Olympia," she told Janet. "You and the boys may as well come and have lunch with us."

"That sounds nice." At least the boys would enjoy some good nutritious food after the less-than-satisfactory breakfast. And she wouldn't have to spend the afternoon dodging Grant Brooks.

The drive to Ever Green Acres was almost a non-event, until the twins spotted the tire sculpture.

"The Tireman. There's The Tireman," one of them exclaimed. "Can we stop for Smarties?"

Janet's response was quick and decisive. "No."

"But Mommy..."

The car slowed, and her father signaled a left turn.

Really, Dad?

No Money Fairy had magically appeared overnight to drop coins in her change purse, so she couldn't be buying even one package of Smarties for her boys. But there was no way she planned to reveal that bit of information to her parents. They assumed she'd sold the Sacramento home and had ample resources, and her pride refused to tell them any different.

"They don't need Smarties," she told her father as the car continued to slow. "Besides, it's almost time for lunch."

Her father's gaze met hers in the rear view mirror. "I'm pulling in for gas, honey."

She peered around his shoulder at the fuel gauge. "The tank's nearly full."

"I like to keep it topped up."

Janet crossed her arms over her chest.

Whatever.

"Can we come in with you, Grandpa?" The boys obviously recognized an opportunity not to be missed.

"You bet."

The car had scarcely come to a stop before the twins were free of their seatbelts and out of the car. Their grandfather followed more slowly. "Anything I can pick up for you, Janet?"

"Milk." Teddy was standing with his hands on his non-existent hips, his face registering distaste.

Bill looked at Janet. "Milk?"

She shrugged. "I gave them diluted canned milk on their cereal this morning. They weren't impressed. But please, Dad, don't feel you have to buy us milk. I can buy it myself."

Someday soon... Hopefully.

The twins returned to the car a few minutes later bursting with the news that their tireman drawings were hanging on the gas station wall. They were also happy about the treats they clutched in their hands. Toni Cirelli had profited from the visit to the tune of a few gallons of gas, one gallon of milk and, naturally, two packages of Smarties.

Janet accepted it, albeit with resignation. She owed so many people now she'd never be able to repay her debts. But the charity couldn't go on. She had to come up with some way to generate income. And soon.

The first glimmer of inspiration came during lunch.

"We had our last strawberries of the season at market yesterday and some clumsy fellow tripped and knocked over the entire display." Verna pursed her lips in displeasure. "I had to throw out almost half the berries, and the rest were too bruised to sell." She sighed. "In past years I'd have made them into strawberry jam, but I just don't have the energy anymore."

Janet experienced a shiver of excitement. "I could do that." She thought of the sugar barrel in Pop's basement and the dozens of empty jars. "I could definitely do that."

Verna's look was thoughtful. "If you had the jam ready by the weekend, we'd sell it for you at the market on Friday and Saturday."

The prospect of earning even a little bit of money was so energizing, Janet could hardly wait for lunch to be over. Ideas came fast and furious. There were many pounds of sugar in that air-tight container in Pop's basement. What about the two peach trees in his yard that were loaded with fruit? Would Grant mind if she used the fruit and his Gram's jam jars? She'd call her products Janet's Jams.

By the time Christa and Grant strolled into the farmhouse late that afternoon, Janet was busily lettering labels her mother had found in the back of a kitchen drawer. Christa immediately began regaling them with the glitz and glamour of the charity luncheon, name-dropping like a bad knitter dropping stitches.

"Did you know Grant and the mayor went to college together? The mayor is really quite charming." She turned to Grant as inspiration flashed. "Why don't we invite him to our wedding?"

Grant was less enthusiastic. "Where are the twins?"

"Out back, under the apple tree." Janet kept her eyes on her work. If she didn't, the way his shoulders filled his suit jacket, his stance with his hands shoved into his trouser pockets, and his dark good looks were guaranteed to generate a hot flash. "Dad's teaching them to play checkers."

Her breath bunched up in her throat when he stepped closer to inspect her handiwork. The distinctive scent she'd come to associate with him—soap and something masculine and lemony—made her light-headed. So much for keeping her distance.

"What are you doing?"

"I'm going to make jam to sell at the Farmers Market."

Janet flushed, unnerved by his closeness and embarrassed by how insignificant her simple business venture must seem to someone of his position and financial stature.

Grant straightened. "That's a great idea. My

grandmother did that for years. She was always giving us some new combinations to sample before she turned them loose on the public."

Janet looked up quickly. "So you won't object if I use some of the jars in the basement?"

"Use them all, if you want. We'll have to haul them out of there one way or another."

We – ? The idea of the two of them doing it together was both tantalizing and worrisome. "Thanks, and don't worry. I'll get the house done, too."

"Do I look worried?"

She didn't trust herself to find out.

An hour or so later, Grant delivered Janet, the boys, and the bruised strawberries to Pop's house. He needed to go there anyway, he said, to check the lawnmower for fuel.

"I'll be back Friday afternoon to cut the lawn," he said. "Anything you have ready for recycling, I can take away then."

Janet nodded. "Before you go—" She hated to ask, but she had ambitious plans and the last thing she needed was for the house to burn down on her watch. "Could you make sure all the appliances are in good working condition so a fuse or something doesn't blow when I'm using them?"

"Good thinking. They haven't been in operation for a while."

When he'd finished checking and pronounced everything good-to-go, Grant produced a business card which he handed to Janet. "If you need anything at all, don't hesitate to call me. My cell number's on the back. I'll see you Friday."

"Bring a truck," Janet called as he headed out the

mudroom door. "There'll be plenty to haul away."

"Why are we doing this?" Teddy's eyes were narrowed and the tip of his tongue protruded as he carefully cut out a newspaper circle and added it to a growing pile on the table.

Janet paused in tightening the lid on a jar of Janet's Strawberry Supreme Jam. She had three dozen jars, and priced at $5 each, they were guaranteed to sell out. The $180 would buy essentials at the grocery store, and if sales were good, she would raise her price on the spiced peach jam she intended to cook up next.

"You're cutting out circles because I'm paying you ten cents of Smartie money from each jar of jam we sell. Remember?" She planned to have her sons give some of the money they earned to Toni Cirelli to reimburse her for the Smarties they'd filched on their first visit to The Tireman. But this was probably not the best time to mention it. No sense discouraging the workers...

A mudroom cupboard had yielded an oversized ball of sisal twine and Freddy was carefully measuring and cutting the string into twelve-inch lengths. His tongue, too, was getting a workout.

Janet carefully wiped the outside of each jam jar with a damp cloth, then lined up her masterpieces on the counter. She stood back and admired the neat rows of jam-filled jars backlit by the afternoon sun streaming through the sparkling clean kitchen window. Once the boys were in bed, she planned to stick one of her hand-lettered labels on each jar and top it with a newspaper cap tied around with the twine. Down home simple. Wholesome. Hopefully unique enough to attract customer attention.

It was no earthshaking leap for mankind, but it was a forward step for her on the road to independence and self-sufficiency.

Chapter 9

Grant checked the cab of his pick-up truck to make sure he had everything he needed for cutting the lawn at Pop's. He was looking forward to the visit, which was ironic considering the many weeks and months he'd deliberately avoided the place. Maybe his enthusiasm was because this time he wouldn't be going to an abandoned, memory-filled house.

He wasn't embarrassed to admit he missed his grandparents. Just thinking about Pop and Gram made his chest knot up. Pop was the only father he'd known.

His thoughts drifted to Janet's boys, Freddy and Teddy. They were missing a father, too. And while he didn't want to flatter himself unduly, he was keenly aware that they were already adopting him for the role. The realization pleased and humbled him at the same time.

Of course, he didn't know how their mother felt about it. She seemed intent on keeping her distance, as if she didn't quite trust him. He had his stupidity at The Tireman to thank for that. In time, he hoped, she'd forget the unfortunate incident and recognize his redeeming qualities.

There had to be some.

The highway was relatively empty this early on a Friday afternoon and Grant eased the truck's speedometer a little higher. He was impatient to see what progress Janet had made on the house. He knew instinctively she was a hard worker, industrious and determined. He'd figured that out just from the fact that she was willing to take on Pop's house. And then there were her entrepreneurial efforts with...what did she call it? Janet's Jams?

Cute name; admirable venture. Gram would have approved.

Nothing about Pop's place felt vacant or abandoned when the truck rolled to a stop on the driveway a short time later. Especially not with Janet's navy-blue Jeep occupying the head of the drive and her boys playing under the big oak tree.

They dropped their toys when they heard him drive up and dashed over to meet him. "Uncle Grant... Have you come to play with us?"

Their winsome grins made him wish play was his sole reason for coming. "Sorry, fellows," he said. "I'm here to work. But maybe when I'm done we can do something together." Grant looked toward the house. "Is your mom inside?"

Freddy nodded. "Yup. She'll be real glad to see you."

Grant felt his pulse hike up a notch. "Is that so?"

"Yeah. She's got a ton of stuff for you to take away."

"Right."

What were you expecting to hear, sucker?

"Catch you boys later."

When he reached the back door, he hesitated, uncertain whether he should knock or just walk in. The house was his, after all. But she was living here now...

He was spared making the decision when the door swung open and Janet stood in the doorway.

"Hi." She swept her wrist across her forehead, her chocolate brown eyes settling somewhere near his nose.

She had her hair pulled back and secured under some sort of bandana that looked very much like one of Pop's red polka dot handkerchiefs. Grant's fingers itched to lift the thick curl that was plastered to her forehead and tuck it in with the rest.

No, that wasn't true. What he really wanted to do was yank off the bandana and plunge all ten fingers into the curly mass. He knew they'd come away scented with vanilla.

Whoa!

He needed to get a grip. These thoughts were totally inappropriate, especially for a man engaged to be married to someone else.

He forced himself to look past Janet to the room behind her.

She moved aside to let him in, and Grant's jaw dropped as he stepped inside and surveyed the mudroom. It was no less congested, but the clutter seemed organized, controlled, somehow. The jumble of cardboard boxes was gone and Janet had sorted the floor-to-ceiling stacks of newspapers and magazines and tied them in bundles.

"You've been busy."

"I have." Janet blew a gusty breath upward to cool her perspiration-dotted forehead. "It may take more than one trip to get all this to the recycling place."

Grant parked his hands on his hips. "We'll know once we load the truck."

He'd used the word 'we' loosely, not expecting Janet to be involved, but she insisted. Freddy and Teddy put in an appearance, wanting to assist too. Fortunately, their mother was able to persuade them that playing with their Hotwheels cars would be more helpful and more enjoyable.

Grant maneuvered the truck so the open bed was as close to the mudroom door as possible, then he and Janet went to work. It didn't take long to settle into an efficient rhythm where he toted the heavy bundles out of the mudroom and swung them up onto the truck bed for Janet to pack into neat stacks.

It was essentially a mindless task that left him with too much time to observe his work partner. He did his best to ignore her long legs in worn denim cut-offs, but it wasn't easy.

He tried making conversation instead. "It'll take a shovel to clean the crud from the mudroom floor once all this is gone," he said, swinging another bundle of newspapers up and onto the truck bed.

Janet huffed the twine-tied package into place. "I'm thinking garden hose."

Grant liked her sense of humor. "Good plan." He chuckled and ducked inside for another bundle.

Janet caught it at the top of its arcing swing and nudged it forward with her thigh. "I've found a dozen or so of your grandfather's shirts that still have some mileage in them. I'm going to wash them, now that I can actually find the washing machine."

"Some shelter will probably appreciate them."

"Do you have a problem with me tearing up the worn-out shirts for cleaning rags?"

Grant looked at her in surprise. "Of course not. Why would you even ask?"

She gave a little shrug. "I know how important your grandparents were to you, and sometimes it's hard to part with the belongings of people you loved."

He dragged a stack of newspaper bundles closer to

the door and heaved the top one up to her. "Did you find that with your husband's things?"

Janet's features froze and the weight of the bundle she was handling drove her back a couple of steps.

He'd obviously struck a sensitive nerve there. Better lighten things up...

"Hey, lady... You're pretty strong—for a girl."

Her expression eased somewhat, and she peered down at him through narrowed eyes.

He grinned, hoping she'd see the twinkle in his eyes. "You know I'm teasing, right?"

"Lucky for you." She wrinkled her nose at him.

He wanted to—

No, scratch that... At least she'd forgotten his intrusive question.

"Do you work out?" he inquired.

Janet caught the next bundle and shoved it into the last open corner of the truck box. "Yeah, I do. Every day. My program is called Herding Six-Year-Old Twins. Wears off pounds you never knew you had." She glanced past him into the mudroom. "How're we doing?"

"Two more bundles after this one. I think we've done it, and we got it all in."

"You can thank my expert packing skills."

"I'm guessing you were a professional mover in another life."

"Or something."

Once the last bundle of newspapers was loaded onto the truck bed, Grant grinned up at her. "Good job, partner." He took off his glove and offered his hand to help her down. He was almost sorry the task was finished. He couldn't remember the last time he'd enjoyed himself this much.

* * *

Janet sagged with relief when she reached the sanctuary of the emptied-out mudroom. Thank goodness that was over. It had taken every ounce of discipline she could dredge up to keep her attention on the work at hand and off Grant Brooks' shoulders and the way his biceps stretched the sleeves of his T-shirt every time he swung a twine-tied bundle upward. She didn't dare linger on his muscled thighs and calves. For a man who sat behind a desk, Grant Brooks was in very nice shape, indeed. No question whether *he* worked out.

She leaned against the closed door for a moment to catch her breath and regain her focus. Thank goodness there were plenty of things ahead to occupy her.

One was staying inside. And far away from any window.

As she expected, the mudroom looked worn and dingy without its cover of clutter. The walls were scuffed and gray with laundry fuzz and dust, and the stone slab floor was gritty with caked mud and dirt.

The washer and dryer looked stark and lonely, their enameled tops stained with smudges years in the making. The interiors looked clean enough, though. Sufficiently clean to throw in a load of Pop's shirts. While they washed, she would attack the mudroom walls and scrub the floor.

Outside, the lawnmower roared to life, and above the engine noise she could hear the voices of the twins. She fought the urge to stick her head out the door and check on them. Grant was there; she trusted him to have a care for her boys.

Turning back to the washer, Janet added detergent, layered in the shirts, closed the lid and advanced the dial to start the water running. Then she headed for the kitchen where a plastic bucket was already waiting in the sink to be filled with water to wash the mudroom walls.

She was reaching for the hot water tap when an unusual hissing noise made her stop and frown.

Something wasn't right.

She followed the sound to the mudroom where water was spewing like a geyser from behind the washer, showering the wall, and puddling in a rapidly-spreading pool on the stone floor.

Janet danced out of its path. Clearly, something had sprung a leak. She needed to turn off the water. But where was the shut-off valve? She had no idea...

Maybe Grant did.

She bolted out the back door and sprinted across the yard to where Grant was slowly inching the mower through the overgrown grass. The boys, she noticed out of the corner of her eye, were on the other side of the yard gathering sticks and twigs into a pile.

Grant saw her streaking toward him and stopped the mower. "What's up?"

"Something's happened. There's water everywhere."

He killed the mower engine and set off at a run with Janet close behind. By the time he reached the house, the pooled water had spread all the way to the back door. His leather sandals hit the water-slicked stone and sent him into a skid that ended only when he grabbed hold of the corner of the washing machine.

Only a few seconds behind him, Janet was not so

lucky. Flailing her arms like a windmill gone berserk, she skated across the floor and barreled into Grant with her nose pressed hard against his chest.

His arms shot out to catch her and keep her upright. For one crazy moment they wobbled together, locked in a tight embrace, the warm water spray drenching them both to the skin.

Grant was the first to recover. Putting Janet aside, he quickly turned off the washer, then leaned into the spray to search behind the machine for a shut-off mechanism.

When the geyser finally subsided, he emerged with water dripping from his hair, his nose and his chin.

Janet, whose senses were thoroughly out of control by this time, couldn't help herself. Where a moment before she'd had trouble breathing, now she burst out laughing. "You...s-should...see yourself," she gasped.

Grant stared at her, open-mouthed, as if he couldn't believe she would find humor in his misfortune. Then his lips quirked in a smirk and laughter creased the corners of his eyes. "Oh, yeah? And you can talk?" He grabbed a handful of her sodden curls and squeezed so the water funneled down her neck.

Her shriek brought the twins to the open doorway. Their mouths drooped at the sight of the adults, up to their toes in water, howling with laughter. "Can we play, too?" And before Janet or Grant could stop them, Freddy and Teddy were stomping and splashing in the water, having the time of their lives.

Sanity eventually resurfaced, and pleasure began a joust with guilt inside Janet's chest. Being in Grant's arms, even for that brief moment, had felt like heaven. As if his arms were where she belonged. But of course, she didn't. It was a totally forbidden heaven. She had no business whatsoever being held by her sister's fiancé.

But this lingering lightness of spirit... What was that? Was she still woozy from slamming into Grant? Or was it endorphins maybe...? From the laughter they'd shared? Or did the warm feeling come simply from the fact that she and Grant shared a similar sense of humor? A humor that, for her, had been squelched down for years.

Janet drew a hiccuppy breath. "We shouldn't be laughing. This could be serious."

Grant was already sliding the washer forward (not a difficult task on the water-slicked floor) to inspect the workings behind it. His voice came muffled. "It's nothing serious. It'll only take a few minutes to fix once I get a new hose. This one's split."

"You can fix it?"

He straightened. "Don't sound so surprised. Has no one told you I moonlight as a handyman?"

Janet arched an eyebrow. "I'd have sworn you spent your days vegging behind a desk."

This was just harmless banter, right? She wasn't really flirting with Grant Brooks... Because that would be a very bad idea.

"Shows how much you know," he said. "Pop taught me everything."

Thank heavens, they were back to reasonable conversation and Janet was determined to keep it that way.

"Was he a banker, too?"

"Not even close. Pop was a lumber man and proud of it."

That would explain the quality wood in the house.

She gestured toward the maimed machine. "Did I do

something wrong?"

Grant shook his head, sending droplets of water floating to the floor on the shafts of sunlight coming through the open door. "This is not uncommon when a machine hasn't been used in a while. The hose dries out, and when water is suddenly forced through, it splits."

"That's a relief. What do we do now? Should I empty the washer?"

Grant spanned his hips with his hands. "No need. It would be helpful, though, if you could get some of this water off the floor while I run to the hardware for new hoses."

"Done."

The twins ceased their stomping. "Can we come with you?"

Grant looked surprised by the request, but not opposed. "If your mom doesn't mind."

Three sets of eyes begged her permission.

"It's okay with me."

"Great. Then let's hit the road."

The boys whooped their way to Grant's truck which was weighed almost to the axles with its load of newspapers. Janet shook her head. That was Grant's problem — —that and the fact that he and his two passengers were pretty much soaked to the skin.

Fortunately, it was a warm day.

Chapter 10

By the time Grant returned, Janet had made major inroads in cleaning up the mudroom. He couldn't believe how different everything looked. Not only was the floor clear of water, it appeared she'd also scrubbed the walls.

As he walked in, Janet glanced up from wiping down the baseboards. "Hi." She gestured to the various pieces of hosing he had draped over one shoulder. "What's all that?"

"I figured I might as well change both hoses and put in new venting for the dryer while I'm at it." He glanced around the room. "How did you get so much done? We weren't gone that long."

"Longer than you think." She discarded the sodden wash rag in the plastic pail and stripped off her rubber gloves. "With all the water that sprayed the walls, it was mostly a matter of wiping them down."

She sounded matter-of-fact, but Grant could tell by the color creeping up her throat that she was pleased he'd noticed her hard work. He found that rather endearing.

"Where are the boys?"

Grant set his toolbox on the washer and selected a screwdriver which he used to loosen the clamps holding the split water hose. He gestured with his head. "They're clearing more sticks and twigs off the lawn so I can finish cutting the grass when I'm done here."

In no time at all, he had the clamps undone and was

discarding the hose on the back stoop.

"By the way," he said, "we unloaded the newspapers at the depot. I told the boys I'd give them money for their Smartie jar if they helped. I hope that's okay with you."

Janet's discomfort was clear, but he figured anything associating him with Smarties would probably do that.

"They told you about their Smartie jar?"

"In great detail, including how you're paying them to make little girl hats for your jam jars."

She pursed her lips at that, creating a charming dimple in her cheek. "Little girl hats, eh?"

"They hope to earn enough money to clean out Toni's Smartie stock."

Janet groaned and shook her head.

"Hey, I think it's great. You're teaching them a valuable work ethic."

"As opposed to letting them steal whatever they want?" She clamped her hand over her mouth as if she hadn't intended to say it aloud.

"You're never going to forgive me for that, are you?"

She shot him a look. "Not for a while."

Understandable.

He gave the top clamp a final adjustment and jiggled it to make sure it was securely in place, then went to work on the second hose. He liked that she hadn't wandered off, that she was staying to watch him work. "They're great kids, Janet. You're doing a fantastic job with them."

She quirked an eyebrow. "For a single parent?"

"Not at all. I'm an admirer of single parents. My mom was one."

"Really?" She held out her hand to take the hose he'd just removed. "I can put that outside for you."

"My dad died when I was a kid, not much older than your boys. My mom worked in a fabric store to support us. I didn't have everything I wanted, but I had all I needed. It was a good life." He positioned the end of the new hose beneath the cold water tap and twisted the coupling until it was tight. "Of course, I spent a lot of time with Pop and Gram."

"Does your mom still work?"

"No. She's retired now." Grant grinned at her across the washer. "She married a really great guy a couple of years ago. They live in Palm Springs."

"I'm glad for her."

"So am I."

"You know, Grant, you're really good with children—for a man."

"What's that supposed to mean?"

She shifted and hugged her waist. "Most of the men I know consider children to be a nuisance. They don't want anything to do with them."

Was she talking about her late husband? Grant felt the sudden urge to punch something. "You obviously don't know the right men." He watched her face, and wondered at her expression. Sadness? Unhappiness?

"You're probably right about that," she said, her voice a little too quiet.

Grant gave the connector an extra hard twist, then hoped he hadn't stripped the thing.

"I love kids," he said simply. "And I've always been fascinated by twins. Weird, huh? I wanted desperately to be a twin when I was young. I remember begging God for a twin brother."

101

A little smile curved Janet's lips. "You might have been a tad late in asking."

"Ya think?" He shoved the washer back into place and pulled out the dryer. "Maybe that's why I enjoy your kids so much."

* * *

The wistful note in Grant's voice tugged at Janet's heart. He had all the makings of a wonderful dad. She wanted to assure him that, soon enough, he would have children of his own, maybe even twins, and that he'd be a wonderful father to them. But then she remembered. Christa didn't want children. How unfair was that? What a waste of love. What a waste of joy. What a waste of a good man...

Sorrow for him and anger at her sister had her grabbing the floor mop and attacking the stone tiles as if her strokes could eliminate the unfairness.

She was tempted to tell him he was welcome to lavish his love and attention on her children, but she bit her tongue just in time. How many times since meeting him had she told herself she needed to distance herself from Grant, not make more opportunities to be together?

The twins wandered through the door as Grant was pushing the dryer back into place. "Mommy," Freddy said, "Teddy and me are hungry."

A glance at the clock on the newly scrubbed wall told Janet why. It was almost five o'clock. Where had the afternoon gone? "Okay, love. I'll get you something to eat right away."

"I hope it's not going to be those stringy green things."

"Frenched green beans. Canned," Janet supplied in

answer to Grant's inquiring look. "Your grandfather must have loved them. He apparently bought them by the caseload."

"No, Pop just believed in being prepared. Think about it." Grant's expression was serious, but she could see a twinkle in his grey-green eyes. "What if the world suddenly ran out of frenched green beans?"

"It would be a disaster for sure."

Grant's laughter made her stomach curl pleasantly. For all her determination to keep distance between them, she did enjoy sharing laughter and witty repartee with him.

"I wish I could have a burger." Teddy's wistful comment erased any pleasure she might have felt. In its place came gut-wrenching regret that she was unable to satisfy her son's simple desire.

Freddy added his plea. "I'd like one, too. And fries. Please, Mommy, can we? I'll give you my Smartie money from Uncle Grant."

She heard the jingle of coins as he dug his hand into the pocket of his shorts. There was something so terribly pathetic about the offer that Janet wanted to weep.

"Hey, Janet, what about it? Let's go to the Grill. My treat," Grant offered.

She shook her head.

"Why not?"

Why not? Because it wasn't wise, that's why not. The three of them going on a public outing like this with Grant Brooks would be downright dangerous...for all concerned.

But when she surveyed the three hopeful faces staring back at her, Janet's resistance failed. Common sense seeped away.

"Why not?" She looked down at herself. "Just let me go change."

The twins' eyes weren't the only ones registering impatience at that statement. "There's no need, Janet. We're all a little grubby. Who's going to care?"

Spoken like a typical man... Her sister Christa would sooner die than be caught looking like Janet did.

Christa...

"Wait a minute. What about Christa?"

Grant frowned. "What about her?"

"Shouldn't we invite Christa? Maybe she could meet us at the Grill."

After a beat of silence, a corner of Grant's mouth lifted. "You've been away too long, Janet. Your sister is not a burger and fries girl."

She's probably not a fan of her fiancé taking out another woman, either.

As if reading her thoughts, Grant gave her a perceptive look. "This is a treat for the boys, Janet. Nothing more."

She turned away to hide the burn heading up her throat. He couldn't have made it plainer, and she should be glad. The brief sentence said it all: If she'd thought Grant taking her and her boys for a meal signified an ulterior motive on his part, she was mistaken. To be even more blunt, he was informing her that any attraction that she perceived existing between them was entirely one-sided, and that side was hers alone.

She should be grateful for that, Janet told herself, because if the feelings were mutual, she would never be able to live with herself.

Chapter 11

Her babies were starting school.

Janet blinked against the sting of tears.

Where had the years gone? It seemed only yesterday that she was bringing two tiny babies home from the hospital (via taxi, since Marty was 'busy' with important clients). And now here they were, the three of them, heading off to the first day of school, her boys on the school bus, she following behind in the Jeep.

It probably wasn't necessary for her to accompany them, but Janet wanted to be sure everything went smoothly on their first day.

She soon discovered she wasn't the only parent reluctant to turn their precious little one loose in the world. Some of the mothers didn't attempt to hold back tears as they gave one last hug and one more lingering kiss before their child walked into the great new world of first grade. At least she wasn't that bad...

The first grade teacher, Bethany Hammond, had obviously been through the drill before. She stood at the classroom door, greeting her new students, reassuring parents, and handing each an envelope.

Janet waited until she got home to open the envelope. When she did, her heart sank. Along with a letter of welcome and introduction was a bill for school supplies. The note at the bottom of the page made her head pound hard enough to blur her vision.

"Payable immediately."

Fifty dollars per child.

How could she possibly give the school a hundred dollars? Jam sales had netted her $180, but most of that was already spent on groceries, backpacks, and a much-needed school outfit for each of the boys. She'd wanted to buy them shoes, too, but that would have to wait. The money just didn't stretch far enough.

And now she had a bill for one hundred dollars.

One hundred dollars payable immediately.

One hundred dollars she didn't have.

What do I do, Lord?

Of course there was more jam to be made, but she wouldn't see returns from that until at least the weekend, and by then there would be other needs, like fuel for the Jeep, personal hygiene supplies for herself. And food for the boys' school lunches. She couldn't very well send them to school with frenched green beans...

Help me, God. Please provide the money I need...

Janet dropped the envelope on the counter and heaved a ragged sigh. What was she supposed to do? And how was she supposed to work with this hanging over her head?

Well, she could do as she'd always done in impossible situations: Lose herself in work. And there was certainly no shortage of that at Pop's house.

With the boys gone for the day, she decided to tackle the kitchen cupboards.

The bank of cupboards occupying two sides of the room were made of solid wood. Janet wasn't exactly sure what type of wood it was, but she liked its rich color and beautiful grain.

At some point in the not-too-distant past the kitchen had seen an update, because the countertops were granite with a metallic bronze fleck that echoed the cabinetry, and the floors were beautifully finished with the same large stone tiles as the mudroom. Classy, but comfortable.

She couldn't wait until the whole house was pristine and sparkling clean again.

Janet pulled a step stool from the walk-in pantry and set it up in front of the end cupboard. Her plan was to sort the contents into boxes for recycling, then scrub out each compartment.

— And while she was doing it, try not to worry about how to pay the school bill. She had no choice but to trust God to provide the money.

Shortly before noon, the ring of Pop's telephone interrupted her work.

It was her mother. "What are you doing right now?"

Janet used her forearm to brush back the damp curls clinging to her forehead. "Emptying out the kitchen cupboards. At this moment, I'm elbow deep in Tupperware."

"Then you're due for a break. Why don't you come and have lunch with me? Your dad is out and I have some garden produce for you to take home. The romaine is especially nice, and the boys will love the new carrots."

Janet was more than grateful for the offer of fresh vegetables, and the prospect of one of her mother's lunches was too good to pass up.

"That sounds lovely," she said. "Give me a half hour and I'll be there."

* * *

Janet wasn't home. He'd suspected that even before he pounded on the back door and peered through the kitchen window. The empty driveway should have been his clue. But there was no clue or reasonable explanation for the disappointment he felt.

He'd been coming out to Pop's place fairly often in the past couple of weeks to clean out the garden shed and tidy up the yard, taking hours here and there away from the bank, even entire afternoons, until his secretary's penciled-on eyebrows seemed permanently glued to her hairline. She was accustomed to her boss being at his desk from well before opening to long after closing.

Grant collected Pop's extension ladder from the garden shed and carried it to the front of the house. It was time to clean out the eave gutters which were so clogged with leaves and dirt that tree seedlings were showing above the edge in places.

He leaned the ladder against the side of the house, and with a big plastic bucket in one hand and a heavy duty scoop in the other, he mounted the ladder and stepped up onto the gently sloped roof. Working aloft would be a lot quicker than continually having to move the ladder, he figured.

Next time he came he was going to clean up Gram's rose bed, Grant told himself as he settled on his haunches and began scooping years of crud from the troughing. If he meant to sell the property, it would go much faster if the surroundings looked good.

And that's why he'd been coming out here so frequently, right?

A niggle of guilt pinched at him. Who was he trying to kid? He couldn't care less about selling Pop's house. In fact, he wouldn't mind keeping it, living in it himself. In the two short weeks she'd been here, Janet had worked miracles with the interior. Every time he came, the place felt more and more like his grandparents' treasured home.

No, if he were brutally honest with himself, he'd have to admit he made excuses to come out here because he enjoyed spending time with Janet and her boys.

Grant slid himself further along the roof and commenced cleaning out the next section of guttering.

So why did that make him feel guilty? Did he fear the warm feelings he was starting to have for Janet were inappropriate?

Were they?

It was true he admired Janet, but surely that wasn't inappropriate. Couldn't a man admire a member of the opposite sex without...without being in love with her, or something?

Of course, he could.

And as for being in love, if he was in love with anyone, it was those two scalawag boys of hers who didn't seem to object to his attention. Besides, if he hoped to be a positive influence in their lives, shouldn't he be on friendly terms with their mother?

Friends... That's what he and Janet were.

Grant banged the scoop against the side of the pail to dislodge a clump of moss and decaying leaves. The pail was nearly full, so he hauled it down the ladder and upended it over the wheelbarrow he'd parked below for that purpose. When the eaves were clean, he'd dump the organic material on Pop's compost pile in the back corner of the property.

He scraped out the pail and was about to remount the ladder when he heard the sound of a vehicle approaching.

Was it Janet?

His heartbeat hiked and a grin split his face as he waited for her to come into view.

The grin faded when the vehicle rolled to a stop on the driveway and Grant recognized Luke Murray, the pastor of Ever Green Community Church.

Luke stopped behind Grant's truck and casually crooked his elbow out the car window. "I thought that was your truck." He gestured with his forefinger toward the bucket in Grant's hand. "What're you doing?"

Grant swallowed his disappointment and sauntered closer. "Cleaning the gutters. Looks like it hasn't been done in years."

"Need a hand?"

Grant and Luke were part of a loosely organized group of men from Ever Green Community Church that called itself His Hands. Their mandate was to be available to community members who needed practical help.

"I won't turn it down – if you're sure you've nothing better to do."

Luke already had the car door open. "What could be more important than helping a friend?"

Grant grinned. "Not much, especially if the one volunteering is willing to do the roof work."

Luke eyed the roof and shook his head. "That honor's all yours."

"Seriously? You just plan to stand around and watch?"

"I might empty your pail from time to time."

Grant chuckled and slapped his friend on the back. "Okay, I can live with that. Let's get to work."

"So how's it going, my friend?" Luke inquired once

Grant was on the roof and crouched over the eaves again.

"How do you mean?"

"You have Janet O'Grady living here?"

Grant stopped scooping and peered over the roof's edge at his pastor friend. Was this Luke his Friend or Luke his Pastor asking?

"She needed a place to live, and I needed someone to clean out the house. Get it ready for market."

Luke nodded. He knew Pop's house well and was aware of its interior condition. He'd been a faithful visitor before Pop got sick and ended up in the hospital. "How's it working out?"

Grant duck-walked a yard or two along the roof. "It's working out great. Janet's doing miracles inside."

There was a pause in the conversation as Luke climbed partway up the ladder to collect the pail from Grant and empty it over the wheelbarrow. After he returned the container, he stood near the top with his arms crossed on the edge of the roof. "So Christa's okay with this arrangement?"

Grant frowned at him. "Why wouldn't she be?"

Luke's shoulders lifted in a shrug. "Just asking." He continued to watch Grant work. "The two of you haven't made your appointments for pre-marital counseling," he said after a while.

"I was leaving it to Christa." Grant had mentioned the prerequisite counseling to her a number of times. Pastor Luke insisted on a series of sessions before he would perform a marriage.

"Maybe you need to take the lead."

Grant looked over at his friend, expecting to see a mockingly elevated eyebrow, perhaps. But Luke wasn't joking. He was frowning.

"Are you sure everything's okay with you and Christa?"

Grant felt his chest cinch tighter. Could Luke read his mind? "You think it's not?"

"You tell me, Grant."

Grant wasn't sure how to answer. To be quite frank, things were not okay where he and Christa were concerned. And it had nothing to do with the feelings he was beginning to have for her sister. There were a number of things about his fiancée that had begun to bother him. One was her fixation on money, though that wasn't coming as a surprise. Christa had made it clear from the beginning that she found his financial status one of the most alluring things about him. It hadn't bothered him before that her self-proclaimed goal was to marry rich. So why did it bother him now?

He knew all about Nigel Chambers, the man Christa had almost married five years before. Nigel was a successful insurance broker who abandoned Christa at the altar in favor of a more willing woman. Christa had insisted on a wedding band before sleeping with him.

She'd had an elaborate wedding all planned and Nigel's treachery only days before it was to take place had devastated and humiliated her. Even so, she made no bones about the fact that losing access to Nigel's wealth was what disappointed her the most.

In some weird way, that whole fiasco with Nigel had Grant backed in a corner. If he ever had thoughts of breaking his engagement to Christa—not that he was or ever would have such thoughts—his sense of honor would never let him do it. He would not be another Nigel; he would not hurt and humiliate Christa. She was too fine for that. Christa was a fellow-believer, a beautiful woman, dignified and subdued, someone he was proud to have on his arm. So why did her preoccupation with his money suddenly bother him?

Unhappily, though, Christa's love of affluence was not the only thing that irritated him. He could overlook her preoccupation with her appearance, but he had a hard time justifying her distaste for handicapped people.

They'd been to Olympia a while back, enjoying dinner at an up-scale restaurant when, halfway through their dinner, the hostess seated a young man in a wheelchair at the next table. Christa hadn't made a scene, but she'd insisted they abandon their meal and leave the restaurant immediately. Her demand seemed totally unreasonable to Grant, but short of humiliating the young man, he had no choice but to humor Christa. They hadn't discussed it afterward. They probably should have, because recalling the incident now tightened his stomach muscles and set his teeth on edge.

He stood to ease the burn in his thighs.

Luke squinted up at him. "Time for a break?"

"Why not?" No point seething up here. Or running the risk of taking out the bottom of the gutter with his scoop.

By the time he reached the ground and emptied the bucket, Luke had retrieved two bottles of water from the trunk of his car. He handed one to Grant. "Good thing I had these in the car. They're for the young people's basketball game at the church tonight. They won't miss a couple."

"Thanks." Grant twisted off the lid and took a long drink of water before collapsing on the grass.

A welcome breeze rustled the leaves of a nearby tree and moved through to cool his scalp. A bird hidden somewhere out of sight twittered its commentary on the late summer warmth.

Luke sank down beside him. "You wanna tell me what's on your mind?"

Grant stared at the distant tree line while he considered how to articulate the thing that was nagging at his mind. It wasn't something he'd divulge to just anyone, but Luke was different. Besides being his pastor, Luke Murray was also his friend and confidant.

He gave Luke a sideways glance.

"Are there ever things about your wife that bug you?"

Luke looked at him in surprise, water bottle suspended halfway to his mouth. "Things about Connie?" Then he grinned. "All the time."

"You serious?"

"Don't sound so surprised. We're human, like everybody else."

Grant leaned back on his elbows. "How do you deal with it?"

Luke took another drink, then recapped his water bottle and set it beside him. He bent his knees and hooked his arms around them. "The first thing I do is share my irritation with the Lord."

"Okay..."

"Then I remind myself that there are probably things about me that bug her. Way more."

Grant returned the wry grin Luke slanted his way. "No doubt. Anything else?"

"Yeah." Luke fixed his gaze on the cloud-free sky. "I ask myself what exactly is irritating me, and why. And how important in the long run is this thing that bugs me? Is it greater than my love for my wife?" He looked back at Grant. "And you know what?"

"What?"

"It never is."

Grant nodded. He admired this about Luke; he was a wise man.

"There's one more thing," Luke said.

"What's that?"

"I ask God to change *my* attitude."

It was good, sound, sage advice that made a lot of sense and long after Luke left, Grant continued to think about it. The more he did, the more he regretted the unkind thoughts he'd been entertaining about Christa. Instead of confronting her and embarrassing her, he needed to be tolerant and accepting. Maybe he'd make up for his judgementalism by taking her out for a fancy meal somewhere. Just the two of them. Christa liked that kind of thing.

In the meantime, he would take his pastor's advice to heart and do his best to follow Luke's example.

And push his fiancée's sister from his mind...

Chapter 12

Lunch with her mother had been pleasant, and lasted much longer than Janet intended. But now that she was back at Pop's house cleaning cupboards, the how to pay the one hundred dollar school bill problem was back with a vengeance.

The Tupperware cupboard finished, Janet moved the step-stool to the next section of cabinet. This one was crammed with stacks of yogurt, margarine and sour cream tubs in every conceivable size, plus more than their fair share of lids. The collection had the maybe-someday-this-will-come-in-handy look, and the only positive thing about it was that it would be an easy clean. One sweep of a hand into a trash bag was basically all it would take.

Janet started at the top and worked down. She was cleaning out the lowest shelf when a yogurt container in the very back corner seemed to resist easy sweeping. It felt heavier than the others had been, and it also had a tightly closed lid.

Janet removed the container and set it on the counter before cautiously easing up one edge of the lid. Who knew what might be living inside? For all she knew, it could be leftover yogurt that should have been stored in the refrigerator months, even years ago.

She held her breath as she eased the lid higher, prepared to see mile-high mold.

What she saw took her breath away just as effectively. The yogurt tub was stuffed with money—an indeterminate number of bills rolled together in a tight wad.

Janet quickly replaced the lid and slid the container to the rear of the counter behind a ceramic cookie jar.

The tub was full of money.

Who did the money belong to?

Not to her, that's for sure.

Obviously, it belonged to Pop Smith. More precisely, it now belonged to Pop's estate — which made it Grant's, and the right thing to do was turn it over to him at the earliest opportunity.

Janet ran a sinkful of fresh water, added some soap to the water, and began washing the cupboard shelves.

The smell of wet wood teased at her senses; the tub of money teased her curiosity. How much was in there?

She forced herself to finish scrubbing the cupboard before drying her hands and pulling the yogurt container from its hiding place.

She eased up the lid and took another peek inside.

The money was all paper. Mostly small denomination bills, it looked like. Ones, fives...

She snapped the lid back in place.

It was none of her business.

She shook the plastic trash bag full of containers to compact its contents, then tied the ends to secure it and hauled it into the mudroom. The next time Grant came by he could take it away. She'd do it herself if vehicle fuel wasn't at such a premium.

While she was in the mudroom, Janet rearranged the bags and cartons already there, and tried to keep from thinking about the money. But how could it hurt anyone if she counted the bills? Just for curiosity's sake, of course.

Who would know?

Who would care?

It wasn't like she intended to keep it...

She made her way back to the kitchen and pulled the plastic tub toward her again. Her fingers trembled slightly as she pried off the lid and pulled out the roll of bills. Slowly, she peeled the bills from the roll and grouped them by denomination.

Then she counted.

The bills added up to exactly one hundred dollars. Not one dollar less, not one dollar more.

An eerie sensation shivered up her spine. One hundred dollars was precisely the amount she needed to pay the school bill. Could this be God answering her desperate prayer?

But no. God's answers didn't involve dishonesty. And it would be completely dishonest to take money that didn't belong to her.

Of course, Grant didn't know about the money. And he wouldn't, if she didn't tell him. What if she chose not to tell Grant? What if she borrowed the money to pay the school bill and then gave him a hundred dollars sometime down the road when she was able? He couldn't miss what he didn't know about. Right?

Janet dragged in a noisy breath and gave her head a shake. What was she thinking?

She scraped the bills together in a rough pile and stuffed them back into the container, angry at herself for even considering usurping the cash. She shoved the yogurt tub into the back corner of the empty cupboard and closed the door firmly.

She needed to get out of the house. Away from temptation.

The school bus with the twins aboard was emptying its cargo of youthful passengers the following morning when Janet pulled into a visitor parking slot at Ever Green Elementary School. In the dark hours of the previous night, when she and sleep were a universe apart, she'd come to a decision. She had decided that using the money she'd found in Pop's cupboard was not wrong. Why would she have found it if she wasn't meant to use it? Especially since it was exactly the amount she needed. It had to be a sign. The way she reasoned it, she'd begged God for help and He'd supplied.

But even as she stepped out of the Jeep and swung her blue denim bag over her shoulder, Janet's conscience squirmed. If the provision was from God, shouldn't she be feeling more at peace about it? More grateful, instead of like a world-class cheat?

The envelope in her purse bulged with the money notes. She would have preferred handing over a simple check, or a crisp one hundred dollar bill. Or even five twenties instead of the thirty ones and a wad of fives. But it couldn't be helped. At least the school bill would be paid. In full. By the deadline. No embarrassing excuses required.

She followed Freddy and Teddy to their classroom where Bethany Hammond was busy placing laminated name tags on strings on the child-sized tables. She looked up when Janet entered the room.

"Mrs. O'Grady... Good morning."

"Please, call me Janet." She pulled the envelope from her bag and handed it to the teacher.

Bethany frowned. "What's this?"

A seed of uncertainty took root in Janet's stomach. "It's payment for the boys' school supplies."

The teacher shot her a rueful smile. "You took me by surprise. I don't think I've ever had a parent pay this promptly."

Janet blinked. "But the note said it was payable immediately."

The teacher laughed. "We say that to nudge parents who would never get around to paying the bill otherwise." She patted Janet's arm. "The end of the month would have been just fine."

Janet felt her chest cinch up tight. She had stolen — yes, stolen — money to pay a bill that could have waited for a month? A month in which who knew what money might have come along by legitimate means?

Shame curdled her stomach.

She should ask for the money back, but pride refused to even consider the idea. It would look too pathetic. She'd let the hundred dollars go, but somewhere, somehow she would find the means to replenish that yogurt tub. She had to. It was the only way she could live with herself.

Face it, she thought as she headed back out to the parking lot, everything was a mess. Her life was a mess; her conscience was a mess. And she was a mess personally.

Not to mention being weak. If she couldn't resist the temptation of a little bit of money, how on earth was she supposed to resist bigger temptations?

Like Grant Brooks...

* * *

Grant shut the door of his Ever Green condo, tossed his keys on the kitchen counter, and draped his suit jacket over a high-backed bar stool. He loosened his silk tie, and as he undid the top buttons of his dress shirt, he noticed his land line answering machine blinking. It was probably his mother. She was the only one who used his land line. Maryann Forsythe didn't like to bother her son at work.

Grant stripped off the tie with one hand and pressed the message button with the other.

"Hi, honey. It's your mother. Tom and I just got back from Greece. I have a thought and I want to run it past you. Give me a call when you have a minute. Love you."

Grant pressed another button and erased the message. He'd call his mother, just as soon as he got comfortable and found himself something to eat. He'd been in a business suit since 6 a.m. and it was now well past 9 p.m. After work he'd taken Christa to an expensive waterfront restaurant in Olympia—the kind she loved to be seen in. The place offered gourmet cuisine that Christa had pronounced exquisite. Grant called it grossly insufficient. He would have preferred something that involved beef steak, medium-rare, and twice the portion size.

But he'd done it for Christa.

Ever since his conversation with Luke Murray, he'd been intentionally romancing his soon-to-be wife. He knew he'd been far too lackadaisical about their relationship in the past, but the truth was, the two of them had never really moved romantically beyond the convenient, handy-date sort of arrangement they'd drifted into at the beginning. Never mind that they were being united in holy matrimony in three short months.

Sometimes Grant wondered how the wedding part had even happened. He knew it was Christa's doing. She had this dream of becoming a rich man's wife, starring as the enviably gorgeous bride in a television-worthy wedding. The rich husband just happened to be him, through no fault of his own.

He also wondered why he'd allowed himself to be pulled along with her plan. At the time it didn't seem so unconscionable. Now he felt differently. But he had agreed, had committed to marrying Christa, and he couldn't back out. He was a man of his word.

Grant exchanged his business clothes for wear-softened jeans and a comfortable sweatshirt, then headed back to the kitchen where he rummaged in the pantry cupboard for something to deaden the hunger pangs still biting at his stomach. Unfortunately, he hadn't been to the grocery store in a while and there wasn't much to choose from. A half-finished bag of potato chips would have to do.

He dropped onto the leather sofa and dialed his mom's Palm Springs number. She answered on the second ring. "Hi, honey. How are you?"

"I'm good, Mom. So, how was Greece?"

"It was fine, but three months there was too long. Both Tom and I were ready to come home."

They talked for a while about the Mediterranean sojourn, then Maryann switched gears.

"I've been thinking, Grant... Now that Tom and I are back, we could come up to Ever Green and clean out Pop's house for you."

The suggestion immediately brought Janet's image to mind, along with an unsettled feeling. It was true his mother had a vested interest in Pop's house. Pop was her father, after all, and this was her childhood home. She might even have changed her mind and decided she wanted to keep some of her parents' belongings, but Grant had no desire to see Janet and her boys pushed out of the house.

"There's no need, Mom. I'm already looking after it."

"You're cleaning the house?" His mother's voice registered surprise. "That's a lot of extra work, Grant. You definitely need our help."

"I'm not doing it myself."

There was a beat of silence. "You're not?"

"No."

"Then who?"

"Janet O'Grady."

A longer beat. "Do I know her?"

"I don't think so. Janet is Christa's sister."

"Oh. I see."

Grant took Maryann's silence as an opportunity to scarf down a couple of stale potato chips. "Janet needed a place to live, and I offered her the house in exchange for cleaning it out."

"Grant... I know what shape that house was in. It's too big a job for one person."

He could tell she was tumbling his news around in her mind. "It could be, but Janet is taking her time and she's doing a great job. You wouldn't recognize the place."

"And you trust this woman?"

She was probably thinking of Gram's fine china and her Czechoslovakian crystal. "Janet is completely honest, Mom. I'd trust her with my life."

Maryann blew out a gusty breath. "Well, that's quite

an endorsement."

Grant leaned his head back and dropped a small collection of potato chip bits into his mouth. "Janet is a widow with six-year-old twin boys."

"Really?"

"They're the cutest little kids you've ever seen."

His mom cleared her throat. "Speaking of grandchildren..."

"Which we weren't, Mom. Seriously, you'd like Janet. She's a hard worker, and besides cleaning out the house, she's making jams to sell at the Farmers' Market. Just like Gram did."

"This Janet person sounds like quite a woman. I think I'd like to meet her."

The thought of his mother making Janet O'Grady's acquaintance filled him with an eagerness that took him by surprise. What was that about? Why should he care whether his mother liked or approved of Janet? "You'll do that in December."

"Why December?"

"I'm getting married in December."

"Oh... Right..." Maryann sounded distracted. He could almost visualize her frown. "I take it the wedding plans are moving ahead on schedule?"

"I guess." If you considered the haute couture wedding gown Christa had selected and the ever-burgeoning guest list. If Christa didn't stop adding names, they'd have to hold the wedding in the Capitol Building. And Christa still hadn't agreed to begin the pre-marital sessions with Pastor Luke.

There was another of those long pauses, as if his mother was processing. "Is everything okay, Grant?" she said finally.

"Of course it is."

"Then why don't I sense that?"

The call ended soon after and Grant abandoned the phone on the sofa cushion beside him. The conversation had definitely been downbeat at the end. No matter how adamant he was that things were just fine, he could tell his mom wasn't buying. She'd always been perceptive that way, and Grant knew the call had left her with more questions than answers.

Unfortunately, it left him feeling exactly the same way.

Chapter 13

The money wouldn't leave her alone.

"Face it," Janet told a simmering pot of peach jam several weeks later, "I am a coward. Plain and simple."

She knew she needed to come clean to Grant about the hundred dollars she'd found, so what was keeping her? Was it the prospect of his reaction? Did she dread how his good opinion of her was bound to change, how any respect or admiration he might have for her would vanish like soap bubbles on an afternoon wind?

Janet gave the peach mixture another stir. Confessing was the right thing to do, so maybe she should be more worried about why Grant's opinion of her mattered so much.

She sighed and laid the sticky spoon on the counter.

She had tried everything she could think of to make herself forget about the hundred dollars, cleaning like a Tasmanian devil and thrusting herself into more and more jam-making. This time it was Janet's Spicy Peach Jam. All to numb her smarting conscience.

It hadn't worked.

Sales at the Farmers' Market were good, but not good enough to purchase their necessities *and* repay Grant. But there was always next week's market, plus the possibility of sales from the jam Toni Cirelli had offered to display at The Tireman. Her hope was to make enough money to hand Grant Brooks a cool one hundred dollar bill—without having to admit the whole sordid story. Just visualizing the scenario had her jamming with a vengeance.

Janet dipped a clean teaspoon into the peachy mixture and sampled the flavor. Last week's peach jam was spiced with cinnamon and nutmeg, both of which Janet had discovered in quantity in Gram Smith's spice cupboard. This time she planned to add a dash of cardamom. It would be interesting to see which combination her customers preferred.

While cleaning out the walk-in pantry the previous week, she had discovered Gram's collection of cookbooks. One book, mostly hand-written, was a treasure trove of the lady's favorite recipes, including many of the jams and jellies for which Grant's grandmother was apparently known. The ones with penciled notations in the margins about their popularity were the ones Janet was cooking up.

Gram, it appeared, had loved experimenting in the kitchen, and her spice cupboard bore that out. It contained virtually every spice known to kitchen-kind, including the cardamom Janet had found earlier tucked between chervil and a container of outdated Kaffir lime leaves.

As she was measuring out the amount of cardamom recommended in Gram's recipe and adding it to the bubbling jam, it occurred to her that in the time it took the jam to simmer, she could sort through the spice collection, discard the outdates, and reorganize what was still viable. She went right to work.

The cull didn't take long. Soon all that remained in the cupboard was a commercial jam tin in the very back corner. Janet dragged it forward and experienced a moment of déjà vu. The tin wasn't empty, and going on precedent, she was willing to bet it wasn't filled with jam either.

She was right.

It was filled with money.

Nearly eight hundred dollars' worth of money.

Janet weighed the money-filled tin in one hand and the plastic lid in the other, trying to ignore the voice in her head that pointed out what eight hundred dollars could do for her. It would certainly refill the Cherokee's gas tank, plus buy the boys new jackets for fall. And it would be nice to eat something besides frenched green beans and tinned ham. The twins were going to need larger shoes soon; just the other day Freddy had complained his shoes were hurting his toes.

Stop...

What was she thinking? This money wasn't hers any more than the hundred dollars had been. It was Pop's money, and now it belonged to Grant. It needed to be placed firmly in his hands as quickly as possible, before sanity entirely disappeared and temptation once again governed her decision-making.

Resolutely, she put the lid back on the tin. Okay, so there was no question she was going to hand over this money to Grant, but would she tell him about her other find?

She should...

But would she? Doing so would amount to admitting she was a thief and a cheat. Then what would Grant think of her?

Or maybe, she told herself in disgust, it was more important what God thought of her.

And what she thought of herself.

Janet glanced at the wall clock. The twins would be home from school in less than an hour so it was too late to visit Grant at his bank today. Besides, her jam was almost ready to dispense into jars.

But she dare not wait too long.

Pop had Grant's work number printed in bold black marker on a small whiteboard beside the telephone. Janet punched in the numbers with a determined finger.

"Ever Green Financial... How may I help you?"

Janet cleared her throat and dragged her palm down the thigh of her jeans. "I—uh—I need to make an appointment with Grant Brooks. First thing tomorrow morning, if possible."

"Could one of our other staff help you?"

If only... "No, I need to see Mr. Brooks."

"He has an opening at 9:30 tomorrow morning."

"I'll take it."

Janet's foot bobbed nervously as she waited in the reception area of Ever Green Financial the following morning dressed in her most businesslike outfit, an ink navy trouser suit with a white waffle-knit shell. Her hair was caught with a clasp at the back of her head and fell to her shoulders in a somewhat controlled cascade of curls. Simple gold hoop earrings added a touch of sophistication.

She couldn't remember ever visiting a bank in Sacramento. Marty did all the banking, and it wasn't until after he died that she realized how weird it was for a modern married couple to have such a one-sided financial arrangement. It pained her now to realize that if she'd asserted herself and insisted on being even a little bit involved, she might not be experiencing her current money woes, and the entire financial fiasco that surfaced after Marty's death wouldn't be happening.

Or maybe not.

She would never forget the shocking news Marty's bank manager delivered when she met him for the first time. "I'm sorry, Mrs. O'Grady, but your husband's account shows only a minimum maintenance balance."

"What does that mean?"

"There's just enough money in the account to keep it open."

She could still recall how her voice trembled. "But how can that be? My husband was very successful in business."

The banker surveyed her with dispassionate eyes. "Perhaps he did his active banking elsewhere."

She'd searched, turned Marty's home office upside down, and found no evidence of other bank accounts.

She did, however, find a key, a key that unlocked a personal post office box containing documents that left her gasping for breath. They were documents Marty had deliberately kept secret, documents she'd brought to Ever Green with her and which her brother-in-law Bart O'Grady would stop at nothing to get his hands on.

A pleasant-faced, gray-haired woman with carefully penciled eyebrows interrupted Janet's recollections. "Mrs. O'Grady? Mr. Brooks will see you now."

The woman led the way down a short hallway to an open door near the end.

"Mrs. O'Grady is here," she announced.

Grant stood as Janet entered his office. "This is a surprise, Janet." He smiled his devastating smile and gestured toward a taupe-colored leather chair facing his desk. "Please, have a seat."

Predictably, one glance at Grant was all it took to

make her pulse trip over itself. Against her will, her mind began fixating on which version of Grant she preferred: the unshaven handyman in T-shirt and cargo shorts who seemed able to handle any household crisis, or the banking executive with his silk tie and designer suit who looked perfectly at home in this high-pressure venue. A perverse side of her said she'd take either...if he were available.

— Which he absolutely wasn't.

"How can I help you?"

Janet pressed her lips together. He probably thought she was here to invest the big bucks everyone assumed she'd realized from selling the Sacramento house. Or perhaps the proceeds from some lucrative life insurance policy when Marty died. If they only knew...

She pulled a plump white business envelope from her bag and laid it on Grant's desk.

"What's this?" He turned the envelope so the open side was toward him and his eyes widened slightly when he saw its contents. He ran his thumb along the edge of the sheaf of bills.

"I found that in a jam tin in your grandmother's spice cupboard."

Grant looked up in surprise and amusement. "You're joking."

"No," she said, "I'm not."

He laughed. "That'd be Pop. He was always hiding things just in case thieves broke into the house."

Well, maybe they did...in the person of yours truly.

"Pop once hid his passport and we never did find it. He had to apply for a new one when he and Gram decided to go on a cruise."

Grant tapped the envelope with his forefinger. "Pop

probably forgot all about this money, including where he put it." He paused and gave her a long look. "I have to admire your honesty, Janet. If you hadn't brought this in, I'd never have known about it."

Janet's throat felt as if she'd swallowed glue. "You can save your admiration, Grant. I'm not so honest. A few weeks ago I found a hundred dollars in a yogurt tub. I gave it to the school to pay for the boys' school supplies."

She dropped her eyes, not wanting to watch Grant's expression alter. Instead, she stared at her fingers which were trying to twist themselves in a complicated Celtic knot.

In her peripheral vision she was aware of Grant leaning back in his leather chair, parking his elbows on the arms, and pressing his tented fingertips to his chin. What was he thinking? Like sons, like mother? That he no could longer trust her in his grandparents' house? Was he wondering what other money she'd found and had conveniently neglected to mention?

Whatever he was thinking, she didn't want to know.

She needed to leave. She'd accomplished what she came for, even admitted the previous theft. Her conscience was clear. Maybe coming here like this would eventually count for something, but right now she didn't think she could stand hanging around to learn Grant's updated opinion of her.

She stood quickly. "I'm sorry," she managed on her way out the door.

Janet took the shortest route across the parking lot, desperate for the sanctuary of the Jeep, When she reached it, she dived inside, buried her face in her hands and let her humiliation bleed out through clenched teeth in gut-deep groans.

How could she ever face Grant Brooks again?

Tears pressed, and she might have just let them spill had not her phone rung at that precise moment. The sound sank her spirits to even bleaker depths. It was probably the school, phoning to say something catastrophic had happened to one of her boys.

She reached into her bag and braced herself for bad news.

But the call wasn't from the school.

It was from Bart O'Grady.

She exhaled through teeth still tightly clenched and turned off the phone with a savage jab of her finger. Nothing on earth could persuade her to talk to her brother-in-law. And definitely not at this moment.

Janet closed her eyes and flung her head against the head rest.

What are You doing to me, God? Haven't I had enough persecution?

As if destroying her reputation and her pleasant rapport with Grant wasn't enough, now she had to be reminded about Bart O'Grady and her late husband's nefarious activities? Would the man never stop hounding her? Would she never be free of his threats? *"Don't try to run, Janet... You know I'll find you. And I promise, I'll have what is mine."*

Her head dropped forward and she pressed her forehead against knuckles already white from their death grip on the steering wheel.

The memory of their last encounter crashed in with hurricane force, Bart barging into the Sacramento house in his typically bullish manner. "Where is it, Janet?" he bellowed, his curled fists plowing into his thick waist.

"Where's the money?"

"You tell *me*, Bart," she shot back. "Marty's bank account is empty, he had no life insurance, and now I find out my name isn't even on the deed to this house. The business owns it! I haven't a cent to my name. I am a penniless widow, Bart. How are my children and I supposed to live?"

She'd already pawned her diamond engagement ring and her high carat wedding band in order to buy food. The utility bills hadn't been paid for three months, but since Marty's and Bart's business owned every high-priced square inch of the house, and she had no legitimate claim, she figured the business could jolly well take care of the bills.

"Look, sweetheart, I have investors breathing down my neck. They want their money and they're threatening lawsuits if I don't make good. And guess what? When I examine the company books, I find that money is missing. A lot of money." He'd jabbed a meaty forefinger in her direction. "Marty did the accounting, so I'm betting he did something funny with it." He stepped forward then and grabbed her upper arm in a painful grip. "I'm also betting the two of you were in it together and you know where he parked the dough."

Janet tried to wrench her arm free and winced when his fingers tightened. She'd have bruises for sure, but that was small potatoes compared to everything else in her life. "How many ways can I say it, Bart? I don't know about any missing money."

Bart's lip curled. "How many ways can *I* say I don't believe you? And if you don't tell me where that cash is, you're gonna be very sorry." His eyes narrowed to calculating slits. "You can't watch those kids of yours every second of the day."

Janet's face blanched. "What are you saying?"

"Just this..." He shoved his forefinger hard into the flesh beneath her jaw and forced her chin upward until the back of her neck ached. "If you don't tell me where Marty stashed the money, something very unfortunate is going happen to those precious kids of yours."

"You stay away from my children." She hissed the words through teeth forced tight together by the pressure on her jaw.

After one more painful jab, Bart removed his finger. "Then tell me where it is."

Janet twisted her head from side to side to ease the cramp in her neck. "I don't know where your stupid money is. I don't even know what you're talking about." She rubbed the spot where his fingernail had bitten into the skin. "But if you ever lay a hand on me again, or threaten my children, I'll go to the police."

Bart just laughed. "I don't think so."

"Why not?"

"Because you're in this as deep as we are."

Janet stared at him. Fear pebbled the flesh on her arms.

"Point the finger at me and you'll go down, too. You were married to Marty for ten years..."

"Eight."

He shrugged. "Nobody's going to believe you didn't know what was going on."

Janet wasn't sure if what he said was true, but the possibility was enough to send her terror and dread through the roof. Especially since she had no idea what he was talking about.

Of course, that was before she'd found the key and

the postal box. That's when the bottom fell out of her already fragile world.

Even now the thought of what she'd discovered in the box twisted her stomach into a queasy knot. She rubbed shaky fingers across her forehead.

If Bart had any clue where she was...

* * *

Grant spotted the Jeep on the far side of the parking lot. He saw Janet hunched over the steering wheel, her posture fairly screaming hopelessness. His heart twisted at the sight. Was her financial situation the problem? He picked up his pace. Hopefully what he had in mind would alleviate some of that and cheer her up.

He tapped on the window.

Janet startled and looked up. She swiped at her cheeks with the back of her hand.

The fact that she was crying notched the band around his chest tighter. He wanted to wrap her in his arms, hold and reassure her. He wanted to tell her to stop worrying because he would take care of her. He'd never let anything hurt her again.

But of course, he couldn't.

He motioned for her to lower the window.

When she did, he jerked his thumb toward The Coffee Stop across the street. "D'you have time for coffee?"

Janet stared at him blankly.

"I need to talk to you about your work at the house."

The shattered look that came over her face rocked him to the core. What— —? Did she think he was going to sack her, kick her and the boys out on the street? Surely she knew him well enough by now to know he cared about her and her children. He wanted to help them.

To his surprise and great relief, Janet gave a resigned nod and slid out of the vehicle.

The aroma of fine coffee met them at the coffee shop door. Grant spotted an available table with two leather tub chairs near a front window and steered Janet toward it with his hand at the small of her back. "What would you like?"

"A vanilla latte?"

The wobble in her voice renewed the urge to wrap his arms around her. Instead, he headed for the counter.

The barista, a young man, who wore his hair in a ponytail, greeted him by name. "Hey, Mr. Brooks. Your usual?"

Grant placed the order, and while he waited for it, he positioned himself so he could observe Janet. He told himself it was because he enjoyed looking at her, even staring pensively out the front window as she was doing right now. He admired her tremendously. Even more now that she had demonstrated her innate honesty. He could only speculate how much courage that had taken.

"Here you are, sir. Vanilla latte and a large black," the barista announced as he set the containers on the counter.

"Great. Thank you, Todd." Grant carried the drinks to the little table and settled in the chair opposite Janet.

"Thank you." She lifted the latte mug to her lips and took a careful sip, but her gaze remained fixed on the table top. Her expression said she was resigned, and waiting for the other proverbial shoe to drop.

Grant's mouth curved in a little grin. He reached inside his suit jacket and pulled out the money-filled envelope she'd handed him earlier. He placed it on the table and used his forefinger to slide it toward her across the well-worn surface.

Janet lowered the mug a fraction. "What's that?"

Grant motioned for her to take it.

She shook her head. "It doesn't belong to me."

"Consider it wages. The hundred dollars, too."

Janet frowned.

Grant leaned back, holding his coffee cup in both hands. "You're working like a slave at Pop's house and I don't expect you to do it for nothing. I was an idiot not to pay you a wage right from the start. This—" he reached over and tapped the envelope "—is a pittance compared to what you deserve."

Janet gave her head another little shake. His gesture was obviously unexpected. Her brown eyes sought his. "Grant, you're letting us live in Pop's house for nothing."

Grant met her puzzled gaze steadily. "Your point being?"

"My point being that I consider that to be more than a fair exchange for the work."

"Well I don't, and in this case it's my opinion that counts."

She was silent for a long time, sipping her latte, but her face revealed a kaleidoscope of emotions as she considered this change in circumstance.

Grant let her process. He had his own emotions to contend with. What he'd told her was true. He should have been paying her from the get-go, and he felt like a jerk for not doing it. Her admission in his office that she'd used the hundred dollars to pay a bill was more than telling, especially since he'd suspected from the outset that she was broke. He wished there was some way to turn back the clock and do things differently. He couldn't imagine the anxiety she'd been living with these past weeks and months.

Eventually, a little smile softened Janet's features. She peeked at him through moisture-spiked lashes. Golden lights danced in her eyes that were as dark and rich as the coffee in his cup. The impact made it hard for him to swallow.

"Thank you," she said simply.

Grant acknowledged her thanks with a smile. It felt good to see some of the strain easing from her face and know he was at least partly responsible. It made his heart beat faster, and made him long to do more.

He settled back with his coffee, marveling at how good it felt to be sitting here with Janet O'Grady. He especially loved it when she smiled, something she didn't do nearly often enough.

He tilted his head curiously. "You seemed upset in the Jeep a few minutes ago. Is anything wrong?"

The smile faded and Janet's eyes became guarded. "I had a phone call." Her fingernail picked at the rim of her cup.

"Nothing serious, I hope."

She shrugged. "I didn't answer it."

He felt his stomach clench momentarily. "Are the boys all right?"

"They're fine."

"Good."

He wished now he'd minded his own business because her smile was gone, and he wanted more than anything to bring it back.

He changed directions. "How's the house coming?"

Janet set her nearly empty latte cup on the table beside the envelope. "The upstairs and the main floor are pretty well done. I'm working on the basement now."

"Does that mean there's recycling to haul away?" He hoped that's what it meant, because it would give him an excuse to drift out to Pop's place again.

"You could say that." Janet's rueful chuckle said it all.

"How about I bring the truck around on Friday?"

"That would be great."

"Around two?"

"Two's fine."

They chatted a while longer, about the house and about the twins' antics. Grant didn't much care what they talked about. He just liked being with her. He wished he could sit with her all day like this, listening to her melodic voice, hearing about her delightful children, watching emotions play across her face. He couldn't help feeling disappointed when she stood and looped the strap of her bag over her shoulder.

"I should go," she said. "Thanks for the latte."

Grant handed her the envelope of money. "Don't forget this."

He walked her to her vehicle and saw her safely inside.

If his goal this morning was to put a smile on Janet O'Grady's face, he'd succeeded in spades. Her smile was ear-to-ear as she gave him a final wave and maneuvered the Jeep out of the parking lot and onto the street.

His own smile faded as he headed back to his office. Nobody had to tell him he enjoyed Janet O'Grady's company a little too much. Nor could he deny how much he was looking forward to spending time with her again on Friday.

Under normal circumstances, all of this would be perfectly normal and acceptable. But their circumstances were not at all normal. He was an engaged man who, in a matter of weeks, would be marrying another woman.

So no matter how much he liked Janet and enjoyed being with her, they could never be anything but friends.

Chapter 14

Grant leaned back in the maple wood captain's chair and patted his non-existent stomach. "That was fantastic, Janet. I haven't had apple pie this good since my grandmother's."

Janet carried their empty dessert plates to the sink and returned with the coffee pot. "Maybe that's because I used your grandmother's recipe."

The apples were from Ever Green Acres. Verna had phoned shortly after Janet's return from her meeting at the bank with Grant. "Are you interested in windfall apples from the orchard?" she'd asked. "They make perfectly good pies."

Janet and the boys had driven out to the farm after school to collect the apples. Thanks to the unexpected 'wages' from Grant, they'd made an outing of it. They'd filled up with gas at The Tireman, dined out at The Grill, and stopped at the grocery store on the way home. Among other things, she'd purchased shortening for pie crusts and French vanilla ice cream to make the pie à la mode. Earlier today Janet had delivered one apple pie to her parents and left another with Toni at The Tireman. Just now, she and Grant had taken a break from loading the truck for some pie and coffee.

Grant waved aside the offer of more coffee.

They'd spent the past hour hauling cartons filled with glass canning jars from the basement and loading them onto the truck. There were still a dozen or so to go.

Grant pushed away from the table. "Before you put

me back to work, show me what you've done in the house."

Janet was more than willing to oblige. She was proud of the effort she'd made decluttering and refurbishing Pop Smith's house. More and more it was looking like the gem it was meant to be.

Grant was suitably impressed. "The place looks great." He stopped in front of the fireplace to study the oil painting above it of Washington Peninsula's Hoh Rainforest. "I'd forgotten how restful this piece is."

"I love that painting," Janet declared and proceeded to describe how she'd cleaned the layers of soot from the painted surface using chunks of white bread as erasers.

She might have known Grant would find humor in that bit of trivia. His teasing only heightened camaraderie that had been building between them while they worked and then shared the pie and coffee. Probably, she told herself, it had something to do with the new understanding and the mutual appreciation they'd gained from the money episode.

If she discounted what happened to her pulse every time he came near, Janet would have to admit she felt more comfortable with Grant Brooks than with any man she'd ever known. Including Marty.

Particularly Marty. With her late husband, she'd always felt like she was tiptoeing around on egg shells, not knowing from one day to the next what mood he'd be in or how he would behave toward her or their sons.

"I'm glad you've left the basics in place," Grant remarked, surveying the living room with approval.

"I've heard that a tastefully decorated house moves faster on the market than one that's stripped bare." Janet drew a wistful sigh. "This is such a lovely house, Grant,

I hate to think of it going to strangers. I'm surprised you and Christa aren't planning to live here once you're married."

Grant shoved his hands deep into his pockets. The muscle in his jaw twitched as she'd noticed it sometimes did when he was thinking about something difficult or distasteful. "I'd do it in a heartbeat, but your sister has her heart set on a place in Olympia with a view of the Inlet." Grant blew out a noisy breath then, and shot her a look that said he didn't care to discuss the topic further. "So," he said with a grin that was obviously forced, "have you found any more money?"

Janet smirked. "Not so far." How glad she was to have the air clear between them and to be able to joke about what had been such a painful subject.

"Too bad. You definitely deserve a bonus for all you've accomplished here."

Janet's eyes danced. "In that case, I'll keep looking."

Grant chuckled. "You do that." He gave the living room one last approving look, then nudged her shoulder with his. "Come on, lazybones. We've got boxes to haul."

The twins burst through the mudroom door just then.

"Mommy, Mommy," Teddy called. "Is Uncle Grant here? His truck is outside."

Both boys skidded to a stop when they spotted their hero.

"Did you come to play with us?" Freddy wanted to know, abandoning his backpack on the kitchen chair Grant had recently vacated.

Grant ruffled the boy's hair and exchanged a look with Janet. She could tell there wasn't a whole lot of resistance on his part to Freddy's invitation.

"I'm sure I can manage that, boys, but your mom has some stuff she needs me to bring up from the basement first. I'll hurry, I promise."

Janet crossed to the kitchen cupboard and pulled out two dessert plates. "How 'bout you two have some apple pie and ice cream while Uncle Grant and I finish loading the truck?"

The boys didn't need a second invitation.

The jars were all boxed and waiting near the foot of the stairs. Grant hefted one. "They're light. I can carry more than one. Load me up," he ordered.

Janet placed a second carton on top of the first.

"One more."

She took her time retrieving the next box. "It won't hurt the boys to wait, you know."

"Don't want them to."

"What if you trip?"

"I won't."

"Sez' you." She very carefully settled a third carton in place. "Don't say I didn't warn you."

"Do people even use these things anymore?"

Grant peered around the three-carton-high stack in his arms to locate the bottom step. Glass rattled when his foot missed it.

"Some do," Janet said, putting out a hand to steady the boxes, "but at the rate you're going, these particular jars may never see another dill pickle. I told you three was too many."

Grant made a rude noise. "You're talking like a girl..."

"That's because I am a girl. A smart one."

"Are you saying I'm not smart?"

"If the shoe fits..."

"Mommy." Teddy's husky voice floated down the basement stairs, cutting through the lighthearted banter.

"Yes, Teddy?"

"Somebody wants to talk to you."

She hadn't heard the phone ring. It was probably her mother.

Grant carefully juggled the cartons as he climbed the stairs. He stopped when he reached the kitchen. "Put your box on top of mine," he directed Janet. "I'll take them all out to the truck at once."

"That would be an accident waiting to happen. I'll set mine in the mudroom, then I'll see what my mother wants."

Grant mocked her with barnyard cackles as she trailed him to the mudroom and put the carton she was carrying on the washing machine. She stripped off her cotton work gloves and reached around the corner for Pop's phone.

"Not that phone, Mommy. This one." Teddy held up her cell phone.

Normally, the twins weren't allowed to answer her phone, but when it was her mother calling, they liked to be the ones to talk.

"Hello?"

"I knew you'd eventually come to your senses and answer your phone." The raspy tones of her husband's twin brother sent a chill down Janet's spine. "Didn't I say you can't hide from me? Did you think I wouldn't figure out where you are?"

Dread clogged her throat. How could Bart know? She'd left Sacramento in the dead of night. Could he tell where she was from her cell phone? Like everything else in her life, Marty's business had paid for her cellular phone service. Maybe that's why Bart hadn't cut it off. So he could track her.

The pie and coffee in her stomach turned corrosive. Why on earth had she answered? Why was she even using this phone? She should have dumped it in a trash bin long ago.

"What do you want, Bart?"

"You know what I want. Where's the money?"

The boys had finished their snack and were already on their way outside, no doubt hoping Grant would make good on his promise to play with them. Janet took the phone into the living room, out of earshot.

"Please, Bart. Why won't you believe me? I don't have your money. I don't have *any* money." She hated sounding whiny, but she knew from experience that being snarky with Bart only made him meaner.

"Maybe you don't have the money with you, but you know where it is."

Janet shivered at the menace in his voice. The other times she'd had this discussion with him, she hadn't known anything about missing money or its whereabouts. Now she did, and that knowing put her in a very vulnerable and very dangerous position.

Eventually she would have to tell him everything. But not yet. Not until she'd sought professional advice.

The best thing she could do right now was to try to sidetrack Bart and buy herself some time. "I showed you the statement from Marty's bank. You saw for yourself there was no money in the account."

"You think I'm an idiot, Janet? There's a massive chunk of money missing and Marty was the only one besides me who had access to it."

"Have you considered that maybe he blew the money on one of his bimbos? But then, you'd know more about that than me, wouldn't you, Bart?"

"Don't get cute with me, Janet. That money is mine, it's out there somewhere, and I will have it. I *need* that money. I have investors breathing down my neck. I've had to liquidate all the assets, and if you think you can run away and live the good life on *my dollar,* you are out of your pea-pickin' brain. I will find you, Janet, and when I do, I promise you'll be sorry you didn't cooperate right away."

Fear and anger made her voice tremble. "Bart O'Grady, I left you everything. I left you the house, the Mercedes, the motorcycle, the speedboat... You even got the artwork, and my furniture, and my dishes. What more do you want? Shall I sell the boys' Lego blocks? Huh, Bart? What do you think they'd fetch? One buck, two? Would that satisfy you?"

The sound of teeth grinding came clearly in her ear. "Lady, you're makin' me very upset. Don't you ever stop looking over your shoulder because I will find you. Don't think I won't. And when I do, you *will* tell me what my dear brother did with the money. Oh, and don't be surprised if one day that school your kids go to calls to say they've gone missing. I'm betting you'll talk fast enough then."

Janet's breath froze to ice in her throat. "You leave me alone, Bart O'Grady. Do you hear me?" Her voice came out strangled and chalky. "Don't you dare come near my boys. And don't *ever* use my children to get to me again."

She smacked the 'Off' button on the phone and hurled it against the sofa. Pressing clenched fists to her throbbing forehead, she drew a series of ragged breaths that were half sob, half scream.

The sound of a throat clearing brought her head up with a snap. She whirled to find Grant standing in the doorway.

From the look on his face, it was clear he'd heard every word.

* * *

Grant crossed his arms on his chest and propped his shoulder against the arched entryway to the living room and took in her stricken expression. "You wanna' tell me what's going on, Janet?"

He could see her struggle for control. Whoever the call was from, it had shaken her deeply.

"Janet?" The single word was more demand that invitation, but there was a reason. Something very serious was going on here. It didn't take a genius to recognize that, nor to figure out that Janet was in desperate need of someone to come alongside.

While he had no right whatsoever to demand an accounting from her, he had the sense she needed to confide in someone. The way she was standing, hunched over with her arms wrapped around herself, she looked as if she was trying to hold herself together. She also looked beyond weary, as if she'd been living too long with fear in her back pocket.

He took a step closer. "Will you tell me what's wrong?"

Janet's head shake said no, but her eyes sent a different message. They were filled with longing, as if the prospect of sharing whatever was burdening her was irresistible.

"Whatever it is, Janet, you know you can trust me."

"If I'm going to tell someone, it should probably be my family," she said finally. "But they wouldn't understand."

"Why not?"

"Because they had to live through my rebellious years when I insisted on making my own decisions and ignored their warnings. Oh, they accept me now, but I doubt they'd be able to hear me objectively and without bias."

He tilted his head and regarded her with gentle eyes. "You might be surprised."

She shook her head. "Maybe... But Dad isn't well. The last thing I want to do is cause him more stress." She pursed her lips. "Are you quite sure you want to hear about the mess I've gotten myself into?"

"Quite sure."

She took a few steps to the side to peer out the window. Probably making sure the boys were occupied and wouldn't be interrupting their conversation.

"The boys are digging worms." His mouth quirked in response to Janet's slight shudder. "They plan to ask Toni if she'll sell them at The Tireman 'to fisher guys.'"

"Fisher guys..." Janet rolled her eyes. "Where do they get these ideas?"

"No clue."

"Probably at school."

"Maybe they're natural-born business types." He raised an inquiring eyebrow. "Like their father?"

Her eyes snapped back to his. Good. They were back on target. For a moment there he thought she might be chickening out on telling him about the phone call. "Let's go back to the kitchen," he suggested. "I believe

I'm ready for that extra cup of coffee now. What about you?"

Her lips pinched together. "It'll take more than coffee to sort out the mess I'm in," she said, but she trailed him to the kitchen, nevertheless.

Chapter 15

Grant pulled the half-filled pot from the coffee maker and brought it to the table where their empty coffee mugs still sat. He poured his black, and added a generous dollop of cream to hers. The fact that he remembered how she liked her coffee seemed to touch her, which made him feel good.

He returned the pot to the coffee machine, then joined her at the table. Wrapping his hand around his cup, he waited until she lifted her eyes to his. "Talk to me," he said.

Janet took a sip of the creamy coffee, then lowered the mug and positioned it exactly in the middle of a cork coaster. She took a deep breath, as if gathering courage for an unwelcome journey. "I don't know how much Christa has told you about my past."

"Nothing."

"Really?" Her expression said she didn't know whether to be relieved or offended.

"I know you were married, you lived in a nice house in Sacramento, and your husband died."

"Four months ago." The dispassionate way she said it suggested there was much more story to tell.

"I'm sorry for your loss."

"Don't be. I'm not sure I'm all that sorry."

"You want to explain that?"

She gave her cup a careful quarter turn on the coaster. "It's probably best if I start at the beginning."

"Go for it." Grant knew he wasn't going to like what

he heard, but he did his best to steel himself.

Janet placed her hands on either side of the coaster. "In my final year of high school, I fell in love with Marty O'Grady. Or at least I thought I was in love. He had a reputation, not a good one, but I thought he was exciting. He didn't care what teachers or other adults thought of him. He was a rebel. His own man. Everyone with a brain knew he was bad news. But I, unfortunately, found him dangerously attractive. I was eighteen," she added as if that explained everything. "My parents didn't want me hanging around with Marty—which naturally only made me determined to keep on doing it."

"Naturally," he murmured, his voice droll.

Janet sent him a quick look. "I tend to be somewhat determined."

The corners of his eyes crinkled. "You don't say."

She sank her gaze back in her coffee cup. "Marty said he wanted to marry me, that he had big plans for us. He was going to get stinking rich, he said, and I was the girl to help him do it. What eighteen-year-old wouldn't have her head turned by that?"

"You believed this guy?"

Janet looked at Grant in surprise. "Why wouldn't I? Marty already had money, way more than the average high school senior, especially one without a job. It never occurred to me to ask where he got it. Turns out he was dealing pot. Not using, mind you. He was too smart for that."

Grant's lips thinned, but he didn't comment.

"So, against my parents' wishes, I married Marty. They had all kinds of objections, the obvious one being that I was too young. But of course, I knew better."

Grant took a slow sip of coffee, trying to ignore the way his stomach was beginning to kick up a fuss. He could guess where this was heading. "So you left town with him."

Janet nodded, her face shadowed by sadness and regret. "We eloped. Had a J.P. in some ratty little place marry us. Marty claimed it didn't matter where we got married because we loved each other. I thought those words held ageless wisdom."

She shook her head, clearly berating herself for being deceived by a smooth-talking snake oil salesman.

"We ended up in Sacramento sharing a crappy apartment with Marty's twin brother, Bart. I didn't like Bart from the start. He gave me the creeps. Still does."

Grant's fingers tightened on the cup. He sensed the story was about to get a whole lot worse.

"I did the cooking and cleaning while the two of them brainstormed for ways to get rich quick. They came up with this scheme where they would persuade other people to put up money to buy run-down properties and we would clean them up, flip them, and share the profits with the investors. At least on paper."

Grant leaned back in his chair, swallowing the sour taste invading his mouth. "Let me guess. You were the one doing the actual clean-up work?"

Janet nodded. "On top of everything else. Until I realized I was pregnant. Then I refused to go anywhere near paints and cleaners."

"What happened then?"

"You mean once Marty calmed down?"

He nodded, noting the note of bitterness in her voice.

"Ironically, the direction of the business changed

after that. Projects got bigger and bigger, investment inputs higher and higher. There were other things going on, too, but I was never privy to the details. Whatever they were doing, the money poured in. Marty moved us to a place of our own. He bought motorcycles, cars—a Mercedes for me, a Porsche for him, the Jeep Grand Cherokee to pull the boat..."

Grant studied the bottom of his cup that had somehow emptied itself. Maybe that's why his stomach felt like it was in full rebellion. "And all this time you were doing what?"

"Caring for our newborn twins and staying out of Marty's way."

"Even though you suspected something underhanded was going on?" He hated his judgmental tone, but everything within him wanted to grab her by the shoulders and holler: *Why didn't you get yourself and your children out of there?*

"I didn't ask questions." Janet folded her hands in front of her and picked at a cuticle. "Marty had an explosive temper, and I learned early on it was safer to stay quiet and keep the peace. The day we were married, we walked out of the court house and Marty said to me: 'Okay, you've had everything your way. Now it's gonna' be my way.'"

Grant could tell Janet regretted divulging so much personal information, but he was glad she had because it gave him a glimpse of the abuse she'd undoubtedly endured. He could feel fury rising within him. If only she'd had the courage, the foresight, to just walk away from him.

He kept his voice neutral. "It never occurred to you to leave him and come home?"

Janet had pulled the blue coffee mug toward her and her finger was tracing the rim. "I was tempted. Many times. But to tell you the truth, I was afraid to. I was afraid my parents wouldn't accept me after what I'd done." Her lips thinned, as if she was embarrassed to tell him more. "And then there was my pride. I figured they'd trot out the old adage. You know, 'You made your bed; now you lie in it.'"

Grant ached for the lonely young woman she was describing. "I think you were selling Bill and Verna short."

"I know that now," she said, "but guilt and pride are powerful deterrents."

"And yet, you came home now."

Janet slid him a quick glance. "Unfortunately, there was a lot more involved than simply choosing to return."

He figured as much.

She was back to picking at a cuticle. "Marty cheated on me almost from the start of our marriage, certainly from the time I became pregnant with the twins. Four months ago, he was out with one of his lady loves. They'd been drinking and Marty wrapped the Porsche around a tree. They both died."

Grant felt no obligation to mouth further condolences.

"It was only when I began untangling his financial affairs that I realized the bizarre state they were in. There was no will, no life insurance, no money in the bank account. Which, by the way, turned out not to have my name on it. Nor was my name on any of the credit cards. It was as if I didn't exist."

Imagining how helpless Janet must have felt made

the muscle in Grant's jaw spasm.

"Turns out that nice house in Sacramento, the cars, the boat, even the furniture and the original artwork, were all owned by the company. Every stick."

Grant frowned as he recalled his earliest impression of her the day they met at The Tireman. "Are you telling me your husband left you penniless?"

Janet ducked her head and abandoned her raw cuticle for a stain on the coaster. "I had a few hundred dollars of housekeeping money that I stretched as far as I could. Then I sold my engagement and wedding rings."

Though it made no sense whatsoever, something about that admission made Grant glad rather than sorry. He couldn't help himself. He reached out and wrapped his hand around hers.

Janet closed her eyes and let her head fall back. "There's more."

Suddenly she pushed back her chair and stood. "Would you please check on the boys? There's something I need to show you."

Grant found the twins on their stomachs on either side of a glass canning jar filled with dirt and some leaves and grass sprinkled on top. It was a worm farm, they explained, and excitedly pointed out a couple of pale pink earthworms snailing their way through the soil. Grant left them glued to the jar, happily watching their wiggly captives do whatever it is that earthworms do.

When he returned to the kitchen, Janet was back at the table working on a large leather purse that she'd turned inside out. She was using tiny scissors to loosen the cloth lining at the bottom of the bag.

Grant had no idea what she was doing, but he watched her work, the tick of the wall clock and the snip of the scissors the only sounds in the room.

When the lining was sufficiently free, Janet slid her fingers into the space beneath the fabric and pulled out a thin bundle of papers. She placed them on the table in front of Grant.

He looked up at her. "You want me to look at these?"

She nodded.

He removed the elastic band holding the papers together and picked up the first one. Unfolded it. Perused the contents.

His eyes widened.

The document was a bank statement. From the International Bank of Freeport, Grand Bahama Island. The account was in the name of Martin O'Grady.

Grant took his time going through the documents which revealed a progression of sizeable deposits made over the past several years. According to the most recent one, the balance was now a little over six million dollars.

Janet spread her hands helplessly. "What do I do with them? Should I give them to Bart? Do I turn them over to the police? As Marty's widow, do I have a legal claim on the money? Or, if it was gained fraudulently, can I be implicated because I was Marty's wife?"

Grant needed to think. He pushed back his chair and began pacing, one hand spanning his hip, the other raking the top of his head. "How long have you known about the money?"

"A couple of months."

"Do you know where it came from?"

Janet shook her head. "I haven't a clue, but I'm

guessing Marty embezzled it from the company. At least, that's what Bart claims."

"As far as you know, your husband—" he hated thinking of the jerk in those terms "—had no source of income other than the business he was in with his brother?"

"I don't know anything for sure. Like I said, Marty never talked to me about his business dealings, and his office at the house was strictly off limits." She dipped her head. "I know it sounds crazy, but let's just say, I found it safer and in everyone's best interest to comply with his orders."

Grant's jaw muscle was bouncing again. "Does his brother know about this?"

"The bank account in Bahamas?" She shook her head.

He stopped his pacing and came to stand in front of her. "But he knows there's money missing and he suspects you know where it is."

Janet hugged her waist and looked so small and vulnerable it took superhuman restraint not to wrap her in his arms.

"Bart believes beyond a shadow of a doubt that I know where the money is. He's convinced Marty and I planned the scheme together." A shudder shook her body. "The worst part is, he'll stop at nothing until he's found me and forced me to tell him what he wants to know."

The reality of what that might entail hit Grant like a fist to the stomach. "That puts you and your boys in danger."

Janet hiccupped a sob. "He's threatened to harm Freddy and Teddy if I don't tell him where the money is."

Grant forced an unintelligible word through clenched teeth and gave the top of his head a violent scrubbing. The guy deserved the same fate as his felon of a brother. If he ever —

Grant took a deep breath to get his emotions under control, then gestured toward the documents on the table. "How did you come to find these? I'm thinking your — I'm thinking Marty didn't leave them lying around in plain sight."

By now Janet was on her feet, too. She leaned against the granite counter for support. "I was searching Grant's office. I thought there might be a will I hadn't found yet, or maybe a life insurance policy, or something. At the very least, I wanted to find out where he banked so I could access the account and take out money for living. But I've told you about all that."

Grant nodded. "You came up empty."

"Except for a key that I discovered in his desk drawer. It was for a postal box at an outlet across town. I drove over there, not expecting to find anything, just planning to cancel the rental. Instead I found these statements. The most recent one arrived a couple of weeks after the accident. The others had been opened, so I can only guess that Marty arranged to leave them there for safekeeping rather than having them in the house. Weird, huh?"

Weird, indeed.

"Grant," she whispered, her eyes lifting to his, "I'm scared."

He could see her body beginning to shake, and it seemed the most natural thing in the world to step close and open his arms. And just as natural for her to walk into them.

Wordlessly, he pressed her against his chest and threaded his fingers into the curls at the back of her head.

With a ragged sigh, she sagged against him and buried her face in the curve of his shoulder.

"It'll be all right," he whispered into her hair.

"I won't let anything happen to you."

It was a rash promise. And an impossible one, he knew. Uttered with a confidence he was far from feeling.

In fact, he was personally so far out of control, he didn't even trust himself. The hint of vanilla he'd come to associate with her was intoxicating. It was definitely her shampoo. He wanted to bury his face in her hair and breathe her scent deep into his lungs. He knew for certain he would never be able to encounter this particular fragrance without thinking of Janet and the exquisite moment he'd held her in his arms.

But that was wrong. She was forbidden fruit.

With a resolve he didn't know he had, Grant eased her out of his arms.

Janet frowned, then stared up at him with a stricken expression. "I'm sorry. I'm so sorry," she whispered, as if she only now realized where she'd been. "Please forgive me."

"There's nothing to forgive," Grant mumbled, though his eyes didn't quite meet hers.

He cleared his throat and shoved his hands deep into his pockets so they wouldn't go rogue on him again. "I meant what I said, Janet. I'll do everything I can to help you.

Do you mind if I take the bank statements? I'm not sure what your next move should be, but I have some contacts who'll know how to proceed."

"Please take them. I'm glad to be rid of them." She hesitated. "And thank you."

Grant headed for the door, but lingering unease made him paused in the doorway. "Be careful, Janet. I've never met this Bart guy, but I don't trust him. And with this much money at stake, I don't think he's going to let it go without a fight."

Janet nodded. "I agree. I'll be careful." Even from this distance, he could see her lower lip quivering and he was tempted to forget about right and wrong and haul her into his arms again.

The moment the door closed behind him, Grant was aware that in the past hour with Janet, something inside him had shifted like tectonic plates before an earthquake. If Janet thought she had a dilemma with Bart and the stolen money, it was nothing compared to the impossible personal tangle he was going to have to unravel if he hoped to survive.

Chapter 16

The month of October had burnished the Washington landscape with vivid autumn tones — mossy green, ruby red and glowing gold. There was a nip in the air, too, a warning that the winter rains would not stay away forever. By contrast, the interior of the Olympia tea shop was cozy and warm.

"This is nice." Janet smiled across the table at her sister. "I'm glad you were finally free so we could have lunch together."

"I agree, lunch with you is nice, but I'm more interested in you helping me pick out my wedding invitations." Christa scrunched her pretty nose. "I just can't decide."

Christa had her Wedding Book on the table at her elbow. It was a journal of sorts in which she was keeping a meticulous record of everything pertaining to the wedding: reservations and bookings, arrangements, purchases, fabric and color swatches, even photos of her bride's bouquet.

Janet didn't know how thrilled she was to be helping choose wedding invitations, but it seemed the least she could do. She really hadn't spent much time with her older sister since returning to Ever Green. It wasn't for lack of trying, but the fact was, they lived separate lives. Janet was busy with her boys, the house, and her burgeoning home preserve business while Christa was wholly consumed with her wedding preparations — almost to the exclusion of Grant, it seemed to Janet. She hoped helping her sister choose invitations would show her support, and somehow ease her conscience about the unwelcome feelings she had for Grant.

She leaned back in her chair and willed herself to relax. Life was good. Right? There'd been no more 'found money' at Pop's house, but regular checks from Grant kept appearing in the mailbox at the end of the lane.

She had mixed feelings about that last detail, because finding money in the mailbox meant Grant wasn't showing up at the house anymore. Mind you, that was probably a blessing given the way she'd thrown herself at him a couple of weeks ago. Did she need any more proof that she needed to be diligent in keeping her distance from him?

Grant must be feeling the same way because other than one rather terse telephone message saying he was consulting with professionals regarding the money Marty squirreled away, she'd heard nothing from him.

That didn't mean she didn't think about Grant. Reliving how it felt to be held in his arms still made her chest ache and her knees a little wobbly. She hated her body's response, but seemed helpless to stop it. Maybe this long overdue time with her sister would help the memory fade, and possibly ease the ever-present guilt.

She gestured with her finger to Christa's personal wedding planner. "What's new in there?"

"My gown. Let me show you." Christa opened the journal and angled it so Janet had a clear view of the picture.

It was obvious Christa had found the gown of her dreams. Going by the photograph, Janet figured it was probably every bride's dream, though not many could afford it. Yes, it cost the earth, Christa admitted when Janet remarked, but it fit her like a glove without requiring one stitch of alteration. That, apparently, made it worth the hefty price tag.

Janet stifled a pang of envy. Her own wedding attire had consisted of a pair of strategically ripped jeans and a rhinestone-studded t-shirt with a sketchy slogan on the front. She wore it because Marty loved its rebellious message and its overall inappropriateness. Recalling the shirt now made her burn with shame. She was sure the person performing the ceremony had added hers to his you-won't-believe-what-the-bride-wore stories.

Janet gave her head a shake. "I'm glad to help you out today, Christa, but I still don't feel comfortable dumping the boys on Grant. I know it's Saturday and Mom and Dad are busy at the Market, but this has to be an imposition for him."

Christa gave her a wide-eyed stare that said: *You're joking, right?*

"Grant jumped at the opportunity when I suggested it. He loves those kids of yours. There's nothing he'd rather do than spend time with them."

"That's all well and good, but shouldn't he be the one helping you choose wedding invitations?"

Christa elevated one slim shoulder. "Grant's leaving the details to me, and that suits me fine. I make the decisions; he pays the bills."

"The two of you are paying for your wedding?"

Christa gave another little shrug. "We're adults, and perfectly capable of taking care of things ourselves."

Exactly opposite to her. Then and now. Janet couldn't take care of anything, least of all her financial situation. Oh sure, there were her jam sales, but what were they in the larger scheme of things? If it weren't for Grant's benevolence, there was no telling where she and her boys would be right now.

"Besides," Christa added. "Mom and Dad can't afford the kind of wedding I want. Grant definitely can."

Janet lifted a toasted almond from her salad on the tines of her fork and popped it in her mouth. "I hope you recognize what a treasure you have in Grant Brooks."

"Of course." Christa dug a cucumber out of her low-cal veggie wrap. "Why do you think I'm marrying him?"

Because you love him and can't stand the thought of living your life without him?

Janet felt a surge of sympathy for Grant. He was too fine to be married simply because he was prosperous and had some positive qualities. He deserved a wife who loved him with every fiber of her being, who loved him for his idiosyncrasies as well as his strengths. Someone who would love him in good times and bad. In sickness and in health. Did her sister love him like that?

Did Christa love Grant the way *she* did —?

Janet's fork fell from her fingers and clattered on the tabletop. The unbidden thought stunned her.

Frankly terrified her.

Was it possible she'd let herself fall in love with Grant Brooks?

She admired him deeply. Thought about him constantly.

Enjoyed his company and appreciated his humor. Marveled at his kindness and integrity. Treasured how he adored her boys, and his gentleness and patience with them. It was no secret she was attracted to him physically; it shocked her how her whole being came alive whenever he was near.

To Have, To Hold

But was that love?

Her eyes glazed over. *Dear Lord... This can't be right. Please take away these feelings. I don't want to love Grant. Not this way. You've given him to Christa, and I don't want to hurt my sister.*

How could she have let this happen? It was totally unacceptable.

"Are you feeling all right?" Christa's voice cut into her consciousness like a surgeon's scalpel slicing through diseased tissue. "You look a little ill."

Not nearly as ill as she was going to be if she didn't figure a satisfactory way out of her dilemma. "I'm fine," she said.

As fine as a woman could be upon realizing she'd fallen in love with the man her sister was going to marry. How could she do this to Christa? She, who'd been on the receiving end of so much betrayal and knew firsthand the pain of it.

"Maybe you don't feel up to the invitation thing."

Janet straightened and tucked a wayward curl behind her ear. "Honestly, Christa. I'm fine. And I'm happy to help you." She deserved whatever pain would be inflicted by helping choose the perfect summons to the event that would take Grant out of her life forever. It was fitting punishment for her disloyalty to her sister.

Oh but Lord, I'm going to need Your help. I can't do this on my own...

Christa had narrowed her invitation choices to four, each at a different shop. Janet tagged along behind her and pretended an interest she was eons from feeling.

"What about this one?" Christa ran her finger over the pearlized paper stock with its classy embossed scrollwork and fancy raised lettering. "Too garish?"

Janet hardly noticed the design. Her attention was fixed on the text: *Mary Jane Doe and John James Smith invite you to witness their shared expression of love as they join together...*" Christa's announcements would read: *Christa Rose Caldwell and Grant* – Janet wondered what Grant's middle name was...

"Well?"

Janet blinked and scrabbled for an appropriate response.

"You don't like it, do you?" Christa held the sample at arm's length and studied it through narrowed eyes. "You're right. It's too garish. Let me show you the next one."

By the time they'd visited all four shops and critiqued the invitation shortlist, Janet's temples were throbbing. With each stop the ache of her misplaced love grew more intense. How would she survive? Was she even capable of standing on the fringes and watching the wedding event unfold, all the while hiding her secret feelings for Grant? And what about after the wedding? The best thing for everyone would be for her and the boys to leave. To disappear as quickly and as unexpectedly as they'd come.

But where would they go? Here, at least, their basic needs were met, and thanks to Grant's generosity, they had a safe place to live.

There'd been no further word from Bart so she had to conclude that, despite his claims, he did not know where she was and would not be showing up any time soon. As a matter of fact, since placing the hidden money puzzle in Grant's hands, she'd been completely at peace on that count. Besides, her boys were happy and well-adjusted, surrounded on all sides by love. Did she have the heart and the will to destroy all that just because she couldn't control her hormones?

Maybe, if she kept a very close guard on her heart, she could get through this. But it would mean no more koffee klatches at the kitchen table, no kibitzing over trash... And it definitely meant looking for a job elsewhere.

It was time to wean herself and her boys off Grant Brooks, Janet told herself as she pulled into the driveway at Pop's house an hour or so later and parked beside Grant's gold Lexus.

She drew a deep breath and slid out of the Jeep. This would be her first serious test of hiding her newly acknowledged love for Grant. She would be friendly and courteous, but aloof.

"Mommy! Mommy!" The twins' footsteps sounded louder than usual as they pounded toward the mudroom from destinations unknown the moment she opened the door. "Look at this! Look at this!" They stamped their feet in a disjointed sort of harmony in order to display the flash of lights in the heels of their shoes.

— Their *new* shoes.

Janet's jaw dropped. "Where did those come from?"

"Uncle Grant bought them for us." Freddy twisted his head backwards to admire the tiny red and blue lights.

Teddy's grin involved his whole face. "Yeah, Uncle Grant bought them. Aren't they fantastic?"

"Fantastic," she echoed weakly.

She looked at Grant who was standing in the doorway to the kitchen, arms folded on his chest, looking extremely pleased with himself.

Suddenly she was furiously and inexplicably angry. How dare he do this to her, just when she'd vowed to distance herself and her family from him? Now he'd sunk them deeper than ever into his debt. "What on earth were you thinking?"

Grant's arms fell to his sides. He looked almost stupefied by the hostility in her voice. "They needed shoes, Janet. The ones they had were too small."

She knew that. All too well. And the truth of it only increased her resentment. "It's not up to you to buy their shoes."

"Come on, Janet. They're just shoes. What's the big deal? Why are you so upset?"

Because you're making it impossible for me to be indifferent... Making it impossible to dismiss you and forget you, impossible to just walk away.

"It's not up to you to buy their clothes, Grant. You're not their father."

Even as she uttered the words she knew she'd wounded him deeply. Hurt her boys, too. They were staring at her open-mouthed, confused, and with enough apprehension to break her heart. The thrill of their new shoes was snuffed out like campfire coals in a rainstorm. Thanks to her, they were afraid to love their new shoes.

Soul-deep regret brought the sting of tears to her eyes. She turned away to hide them.

And she'd thought her life was a mess before?

Behind her, she heard Grant say a quiet goodbye to the twins.

Then the door closed.

With her frayed heart holding together by mere threads, she forced herself to prepare a meal that none of them wanted. The threads pulled even thinner at bedtime when Teddy asked, his voice full of trepidation: "Mommy, is it okay if we thank God for our new shoes?"

The thread finally snapped when, as she was leaving their bedroom after tucking them in and kissing them goodnight, she heard Freddy murmur to his brother, "I wish Uncle Grant *was* our daddy."

"Me, too," Teddy said sadly.

Unspeakable grief consumed Janet as she stumbled down the stairs, her arms wrapped tightly around herself to hold her shredded heart in place.

That made three of them.

Chapter 17

"**Tell** me what you think of these." Janet handed Toni a re-sealable bag of cinnamon-spiced dried apple rings.

Toni pulled a leathery ring from the bag and took a bite. She chewed thoughtfully. "These are good, Janet. Really good."

"I found a dehydrator in Pop's basement. I thought if you liked them, maybe we could try selling some here at The Tireman."

Toni reached for another of the cinnamon-flavored snacks. "Absolutely. How many bags did you bring?"

"Two dozen."

"I predict they'll be gone in a flash. Oh, and can you bring me more of your apple butter? I have to tell you, Janet's products are really catching on."

That was good news. Janet needed all the sales she could get. Especially if she ever hoped to be independent of Grant's benevolence.

"D'you have time for coffee?"

"Sure."

One of the happy by-products of coming back to Ever Green was the fact that she and Toni had become fast friends. Sharing a cup of coffee was something Janet looked forward to whenever she could manage a visit to The Tireman, which was happening with satisfying frequency thanks to the popularity of her homemade products. She'd taken advantage of the break from rain today to walk over with the dried apple snacks.

As she accepted a china mug filled with cream-laced

coffee, Janet noted Toni's dour expression. "Something bothering you?"

Toni shrugged. The corners of her mouth dipped.

"You can tell me, you know."

Toni's breath whistled through her teeth. "I had a date last night. Finally." She dropped into the chair opposite Janet's with a flounce that personified an exclamation point. "There's this guy who's been stopping in at The Tireman for the past couple of weeks. He's not from around here, though his grandfather lives in the area." Toni clenched her molars and pinched her lips together as if the information was leaking out against her will. "Last week he asked if he could take me out for coffee."

"And — ?"

"He's cute and seemed really nice, so I said yes. Turns out he's a loser. All he wanted was information on who in the Ever Green community might be thinking of selling their property." Toni spread her fingers wide in frustration. "He had no interest in me personally. He might even be married, for all I know. I hate men like that."

"Me, too. I'm so sorry, Toni."

"Aren't there any nice guys out there?"

Yes, there are, Janet wanted to say, but the only one who came to mind was the ultimate in not available — to Toni, to herself, or to any other woman with the exception of her sister Christa. And what frustrated Janet about that was that her sister didn't seem to appreciate or cherish the guy anywhere near how she should. Grant deserved so much more. Just thinking about it made her chest clench tight with longing and loss, and the injustice of it all.

The tick of the old-fashioned clock on the wall and the occasional swish of vehicle tires on the pavement outside the gas station were the only sounds in the little backroom office for several minutes as each woman considered the hopeless state of her love life.

Suddenly Janet inhaled sharply. *Enough of that.*

"I think I'm about done cleaning out Pop's house," she said. It wasn't the most scintillating of conversation topic changes, but she hoped it might shift her unhappy thoughts away from Grant Brooks. "I've kept back enough of the contents for it still to be a fully functioning house."

The truth was she didn't have the heart to dispose of all the truly lovely items like Gram's Waterford crystal and her fine china dishes which were now freshly washed and artfully displayed behind the sparkling glass doors of the china cabinet. "Grant and Christa can decide what to do with what's left once the house sells."

"Speaking of the bride and groom, what's new on the wedding front?"

To Janet's mind, the subject of brides, grooms and weddings was no more palatable than Toni's unsatisfactory date. As much as possible, she avoided thinking about her sister's marriage. It made her feel too sad, too lost, as if her world were ending.

It was interesting, she reflected , that regardless of how many times Marty had disappointed her, cheated on her with other women, inexcusably let her down, she'd never felt this empty and abandoned. Maybe that's because she'd never truly loved Marty. Certainly hadn't loved him the way she loved Grant.

It wasn't that Grant had invited her affection or given any indication he felt the same way about her.

He'd never been anything but kind, thoughtful and encouraging, friendly and considerate, and generous beyond expectation. Not once had he been disloyal to Christa in any way, unless you counted the time he'd put his arms around her when she'd virtually thrown herself at him. Her cheeks burned at the memory.

No, Grant had never made inappropriate advances. Anything remotely romantic had come from her, which was why she had to put an end to this ridiculous infatuation. It wouldn't be easy. It would be hard enough to break her own attachment; she couldn't imagine how painful it would be for her boys. But she was working on it.

One of the ways she was finding to cope was focusing on the daily practicals. She'd lost count of the number of times she'd given herself the stern lecture: *Grant is marrying Christa. It's reality. Accept it. Get over it. Your sister deserves a beautiful wedding, and your full support. Make it happen, no matter how hard that is.*

She was startled from her introspection at the sound of Toni's voice. "Hello... Where did you go?"

Janet shook her head to clear it. "Nowhere important. You asked about the wedding?" Cradling the china coffee mug in both hands, she took a slow sip. "Well, my dress is purchased." Phrasing it that way made it seem less personal somehow. Christa had chosen the dress; Christa had paid for it. More specifically, Grant's credit card had paid for it, but dwelling on that detail only complicated things more in her head.

"What's it like?"

"The dress? It's ivory silk crepe." Janet outlined a deep shoulder to shoulder scoop. "Crumb-catcher neckline. The rest is fairly fitted. Floor length. Little fabric-covered buttons all up the back. Very elegant."

"It sounds lovely."

It *was* rather lovely, Janet was forced to admit. It was thanks to Christa who had an eye for what looked good. Janet's only regret was that she would be wearing the dress to officially usher out of her life the man she loved.

Change the subject...

"I think I may have found a job."

This statement definitely snagged Toni's attention. Both bird-wing eyebrows rose. "Where?"

"With a maid service in Olympia...Ever Clean. They're looking for people to do housecleaning in clients' homes. It's a bit of a drive, but the woman who owns the business is very accommodating. She's willing to let me work during the hours the boys are in school."

Toni regarded her over the rim of her cup. "Well, no one will give you a better recommendation than Grant Brooks, that's for sure. To hear him talk, the world spins on its axis because of Janet O'Grady. The way he talks about you, I sometimes wonder if he's marrying the wrong Caldwell."

Unwanted color bloomed in Janet's cheeks. No way was she going to respond to that.

"The job will mean the boys and I can get our own place. Nothing fancy. Maybe an apartment in Olympia, though the boys aren't keen on the idea. They love Pop's house." She dipped her head. "So do I, quite frankly."

"Has Grant asked you to leave?"

"No, but it's better that we do." When Toni looked like she might refute that, Janet added quickly, "Grant's been wonderful to let us stay at the house this long, but everyone knows it's a bad idea to presume on a friendship."

"Oh!" Toni straightened suddenly. "Speaking of friends—" She gave her head a tap with the palm of her hand. "Blame it on my disastrous date last night. Did your friend find you?"

Coffee sloshed out of the china mug and onto Janet's jean-clad thigh. "My friend—?" She dug a crumpled tissue from the pocket of her jeans and pressed it against the dampness.

"From Sacramento. He stopped in yesterday asking about you."

Janet's mental antennae shot up a foot in the air. Apprehension clumped her blood. She had no friends in Sacramento.

"A man?"

"Driving a lovely dark red Mercedes."

Bart. Driving her car.

"He wanted to know where you lived."

The china mug clattered onto the coffee table. "I hope you didn't tell him."

"I'm sorry, Janet. I did." Consternation contorted Toni's features. "Is that a problem?"

"I have to go, Toni." She shot to her feet and bolted out the door with Toni trailing behind.

"I hope I didn't make trouble for you..."

Janet didn't say so, but she feared that might be the understatement of the year.

* * *

Grant tipped back in his chair and twirled a pencil between his fingers as he studied the intermittent raindrops making wavy trails down the outside of his office window. The sky pressed in with layers of iron-gray cloud.

He might as well have taken the day off for all the good he was doing here at the bank. Good thing he was the boss or he'd be fired, for sure. It'd been like this for almost two weeks. Ever since Janet threw him out of her house.

At least, that's what it felt like.

He'd been annoyed at first. Angry, resentful, with an in-your-face, after-all-I've-done-for-her attitude. But that fizzled out pretty quickly when he considered all she'd been through and the worries she was still carrying. Worries he'd promised in a moment of weakness to handle, but in reality could do nothing about.

He still didn't know what she was so steamed about. He'd been puzzling on that for days. It had to be about more than the shoes he'd bought the boys. It made his heart hurt all over again to recall how the twins' over-the-moon joy had been snuffed out in an instant by Janet's biting remark.

He tapped the pencil on the chair arm, beating out a frustrated rhythm, then threw it on the desk and slumped in his chair. He leaned his head against the padded back and closed his eyes, revisiting that moment, remembering the way she'd looked. The color in her cheeks, the fire in her eyes.

Even indignant, Janet was gorgeous. And stubborn. She was trying so hard to be in control of her life. And the harder she tried, the more he wanted to tell her to just stop and let him protect her. He longed to—

Whoa-o... Aren't you forgetting something, boy-o?

Grant groaned.

He had no business having thoughts like that about

Janet. Christa should be forefront in his mind. But lately, whenever he thought about Christa, all he felt was guilt. As if he was already being an unfaithful spouse.

Not for the first time he tried to visualize what life would be like once he and Christa were married, but his thoughts quickly meandered back to Janet. Why was that?

Perhaps more important, did he actually know what he felt for Janet?

He enjoyed her company immensely. They had an easy, pleasant camaraderie. She was incredibly loving; it fairly oozed from her being. The love she had for her boys was so intense it sometimes made him weak in the knees thinking about it. He loved being with Janet, loved looking at her, loved watching her expressive face. Loved seeing her beautiful brown eyes warm to liquid molasses. He found her clean wholesomeness deeply appealing.

Grant brought his fingers to his nose. Even now, he imagined he could smell the lingering fragrance of her hair on them...

He straightened so suddenly his office chair lurched forward and slammed his ribs against the front edge of his desk. This train of thought was taking him nowhere good. He needed to disembark pronto and to get a grip on himself. He was marrying Christa, and he needed to remind himself that when they'd made that commitment, he had also made the conscious decision to be whatever she needed.

Grant raked his fingers through his hair. Of course, that decision was made a long time ago, before —

But no. He couldn't...wouldn't renege. Christa was a classy lady; she deserved more.

A quick tap on his office door announced the entrance of his secretary.

He frowned at the intrusion.

"I'm sorry to interrupt you, Grant, but there's a call for you."

"I asked you to hold my calls."

"I know," she said, "but I thought you might want to take this one. It's from Toni Cirelli. She says it's personal, and extremely urgent."

* * *

Janet took the half-mile from The Tireman to Pop's house at a run, casting frequent glances over her shoulder. The burn in her stomach and the tightness in her chest had nothing to do with any lack of fitness.

Somehow Bart had found her. She'd tried to convince herself that his threats to harm her children were hollow and obsolete, but hearing the threat was in her neighborhood, almost on her doorstep, was another matter altogether. She didn't know how he'd tracked her down.

Why was no mystery. He wanted the missing money.

Maybe she should just tell him where it was. There was no doubt in her mind the funds in the Bahamas were embezzled from the company. What did it matter to her if they weren't legitimate earnings?

But ah, there was the rub. It did matter. Bart had already admitted that he and Marty weren't completely honest in all their business dealings and that she could be implicated. At this point, though, with Bart breathing down her neck, she would willingly turn over the Bahamian bank statements if it meant he would leave her and her boys alone.

Of course, she wasn't able to turn them over because Grant had them. Bart would be livid if he learned that.

Janet ran on, her calves burning and the soles of her feet throbbing from pounding on the pavement.

She was almost at Pop's house when the drizzle turned to rain. She pulled the hood of her jacket forward and stuffed her curly mane inside. The wetness only added to her discomfort and heightened her sense of impending doom.

She saw the car on the driveway long before she started up the lane. It was her car, all right. Her cardinal red S-Class Mercedes. Apparently Bart was driving it now. So what had happened to his claim of liquidating company-owned assets to pay out investors?

The temptation was strong to make a quick deke into the woods hedging the property and postpone the confrontation with her former brother-in-law, but what would that gain? She'd just be avoiding the inevitable. Now that he'd found her, Bart would not be going away.

Her steps slowed.

Help me, Father. And protect my boys...

She was almost even with the house when she spotted him. Bart rose from one of the wicker chairs on the veranda and moved to the head of the porch stairs. He stood there, hands on hips, waiting for her, looking inordinately pleased with himself.

He'd shaved his head, she noticed. An attempt to heighten the Intimidation Index?

She fingered the key in her pocket. Thank goodness the house was locked. She hated the idea of Bart snooping through Pop's house.

He waited until the last second to step aside and let

her pass.

Janet swept the hood from her head in a weary gesture. "How did you find me, Bart?"

His grin was smug. "Wasn't hard. Where else would a penniless female run but home?" His expression hardened as he made a survey of the house and manicured grounds. "I have to ask myself, how does a woman who claims to have no money afford to live in a place like this?" His features twisted unpleasantly. "Could it be that you have money after all, Janet? Money that you and my traitor-of-a-brother stole from me?" He gave her an angry shove that sent her tumbling backwards into one of the wicker chairs. "Please don't insult my intelligence by trying to deny it," he snarled.

Janet steeled the tremor from her voice; Bart must not know how nervous she was. It was probably a good thing she wasn't standing or he'd see her legs wobbling like poorly-set Jell-O. "I do deny it, Bart. This is not what it looks. The house belongs to a—a friend who's letting me stay here."

Bart stepped closer until he was looming over her. Anger painted his face with florid color. "Don't lie to me. I'm not stupid." He swept his fleshy hand back as if he meant to strike her. "The truth, Janet. Now, or you'll be sorry."

She flinched and braced for the blow, her mind flashing to the twins and Bart's threats of harm to them. She cast a surreptitious glance at her watch. Thank goodness, it wasn't yet time for school dismissal. The boys were still safe in their first grade classroom with Bethany Hammond.

Bart saw her glance and smirked. His hand dropped. "Yeah, you should worry about those kids of yours. I did some investigating. Checked out their school. Hammond— Isn't that the teacher's name?"

Janet felt the color drain from her face.

"Did you know there's practically no security at that place? I saw your boys out in the schoolyard." He touched a finger to his chin and narrowed his eyes. "Blue jeans and matching red hoodies... Isn't that what they were wearing?"

A wave of very real fear iced its way down her spine. Bart wasn't bluffing. He had seen her boys.

For a moment, her brain went numb, incapable of function or thought, though she was vaguely aware of birds exchanging greetings nearby and a vehicle motor off in the distance. If only it was coming to rescue her, or maybe to speed her away with her children, whisking them off to safety somewhere else. But where could she find a place that was safer than this?

"I'm waiting."

Janet forced herself to focus. If she got inside the house, maybe she could snag her car keys and somehow slip away from Bart. She'd drive to the school, collect her kids, and disappear.

But no. Bart would never let that happen.

If she got to her cell phone, though, she could call someone for help. But who would she call? Her father? Probably not. An encounter with Bart would most likely kill him. Grant? After the episode with the shoes, they weren't exactly on the best of terms. And besides, this wasn't his war. It was enough she'd burdened him with the secret bank account problem.

Unfortunately both options were out of the question because she was on the porch and her phone and car keys were inside the house. On the kitchen counter.

If only she'd thought to write down the number of the off-shore bank account. She'd give it to Bart in a heartbeat. Justice was the last thing on her mind right now. Nothing was worth jeopardizing her boys' safety.

Think, Janet...

She dropped her hands to her thighs and heaved a deep sigh that she hoped sounded like resignation. "All right, Bart," she said, "you win."

He took a step backward so she could get to her feet, but his narrowed eyes said he didn't quite trust this sudden change of heart.

"The information you want is inside," she said, moving toward the front door. She brought the key out of her pocket and slid it into the lock.

She would have slipped through the open door and slammed it in his face, but Bart grabbed her arm. "Not so fast. I'm coming with you. And in case you have any thoughts about running? Forget them."

Her heart sank. Was she so obvious?

From the front foyer, she could see her cell phone on the granite kitchen counter. If she could just get to it, all it would take was a couple of seconds.

Lord – ?

The opportunity came when Bart halted in the entry to scan the interior of the house. In particular, the living room with its gracious furnishings and decor. Janet saw her chance, and without considering the consequences, she spun around, cocked her leg and slammed a hard kick at Bart's right knee.

He swore viciously and grabbed his knee with both hands.

The pain in her own foot was unexpected, but Janet didn't let it stop her. She sprinted to the kitchen, snatched up her cell phone and dived into the pantry, punching the school's number on speed dial as she went. She clamped the phone to her ear with one hand and shoved the pantry door shut with the other, effectively enclosing herself in darkness. A strip of light under the door allowed her to locate the collapsible step stool and wedge it under the knob. Only then did she flip on the light switch.

By this time, Bart had recovered enough to reach the pantry door where he alternately cursed and tried to force the door open.

"Ever Green Elementary. Sorry it took so long..." It was the new receptionist—a young girl, working her first job.

Janet tried to calm her ragged breathing. "This is Janet O'Grady. My boys, Freddy and Teddy, are in Bethany Hammond's class."

"Oh, the twins... Freddy and Teddy... I just love their names. And they're *so* cute..."

Janet wanted to scream at the girl; an enraged monster was about to break the door down.

"Listen," she said curtly, "this is an emergency. Do not, under any circumstances, allow my boys to leave the school. Make sure they stay there. Do you hear me?"

The wooden pantry door was vibrating under the pressure of Bart's shoulder, and the noise of his bellowed threats was so loud she had to strain to hear the receptionist's response—timid now, and uncertain.

"I'm terribly sorry, Mrs. O'Grady, but the twins aren't here."

"What?" Janet's exclamation was off the volume scale. "Where are they? Did someone take them? Who?"

"I'm new here, Mrs. O'Grady. I'm afraid I don't

know his name."

"His — ?"

Her head felt ready to explode.

Chapter 18

"**I'm** sure Mrs. Hammond wouldn't release your boys to a stranger, Mrs. O'Grady," the school secretary attempted to reassure her. "If you'll just hold on a minute, I'll..."

But Janet wasn't listening anymore. She already knew what had happened. Bart had taken them.

Bart, who had now switched from using his shoulder to trying to smash the door in with his foot.

Fury more fierce than anything she'd ever experienced raced on jet fuel through her body. She shoved aside the step stool, and just as Bart was making one more run at the door, she yanked it open so abruptly that he fell headlong into the pantry, upending the bottom shelf and bringing down an avalanche of tinned goods on his sprawled body. Who'd have thought she'd be this grateful for frenched green beans?

Acting on instinct, Janet snatched up the only weapon she could find, a string floor mop propped in the corner, and began clobbering Bart with it.

"What have you done with my boys?" she screamed between blows. "Where are they?"

"What are you talking about? Ow! Stop it," Bart bawled, curving his beefy arms over his head to protect himself. "I'm warning you, Janet, stop it right now or you'll be sorry."

"*You'll* be sorry if you've hurt my children." She took a straight-armed swing as wide as the narrow confines of the pantry would allow and brought the mop head hard against his left ear to emphasize her point.

Bart hollered in pain and clutched at his ear with one hand while grabbing a handful of mop strings with the other.

Janet let the mop fall. He'd taken her boys. What had he done with them? Were they in the car, maybe? Locked inside?

She dashed through the kitchen, bolted out the mudroom door, and headed for the Mercedes parked on the driveway.

It was still raining, though the squall had settled back into a fine drizzle again. Janet skidded to a stop at the car and swiped moisture from the windows with her sleeve. She peered inside, first through the front window, then through the back. All she saw was a crumpled potato chip bag and a Big Gulp container. There was no sign of the twins.

Surely Bart wasn't heartless enough to have locked them in the trunk...

"Freddy! Teddy! It's Mommy." She pounded on the trunk lid with her fist, hoping if the boys were inside that one of them would answer. Let her know they were alive. Unharmed.

All she heard was silence.

Oh God, no...

Fear and dread welled up so strong it made her nauseous. What had he done to them? She had to know. She had to see inside the trunk.

Mercifully, the car was unlocked. She yanked open the driver's side door and dove inside, fumbling for the trunk release.

"What do you think you're doing?" Still cursing, Bart grabbed the back of her jacket and hauled her backwards out of the car.

Janet stumbled, twisted. Her fingers curved into claws that reached for his face. "Where are they?" she shouted. "What have you done with them?"

Before she could make contact with his face, Bart caught her wrists and held them tightly. At the same time he took a wary step backward. "You're out of your mind! I don't have a clue what you're talking about."

Janet struggled like a woman possessed to wrench herself free of his grasp.

"You kidnapped my boys."

"You're crazy!" Bart pinned her wrists in one hand and landed a stinging slap on her cheek with the other.

The blow shocked Janet into stunned immobility and Bart used the moment to turn her around, hook his elbow around her neck and pull her back against him.

"You are making me very upset," he growled in her ear. His forearm pressed against her throat so hard she could scarcely breathe. "Why are you making this so difficult? All I want is for you to tell me where the money is."

He could talk about money when her boys' lives were in jeopardy? Desperate and furious, Janet grabbed at his forearm with both hands and pried it away from her throat enough to croak, "If you've done anything to hurt my boys, I swear, Bart O'Grady, I will kill you with my bare hands!"

Bart snickered at her wheezy threat. "That I'd like to see."

"And if she doesn't, I will."

* * *

The sight of Janet, imprisoned in a hammerlock by a

burly bald guy — who had to be Bart O'Grady — sent rage rocketing through Grant's body. His only thought was that he had to save Janet. Free her from the grip that had her wild-eyed with terror.

Was the guy planning to choke her?

Not on his watch.

Or was it already too late? He'd seen Janet slump right about the time he'd added his warning to hers.

Grant wanted nothing more than to make a flying tackle and take the guy down, but that wouldn't help Janet...

He forced himself to remain calm.

"Let her go."

For a moment, he thought Bart would refuse. Then, amazingly, the man complied.

The instant the pressure against her throat eased, Janet tore Bart's arm away and dived toward Grant. She grabbed a handful of his striped dress shirt and lifted anguish-filled eyes to his. "He has the boys, Grant." The words came out choked and raspy. "He kidnapped my boys."

Grant wrapped his arm around her and brought her close to his chest. His heart was thudding so violently he could hardly speak.

"No, he didn't, honey. The boys are safe. They're at your mom's."

She tipped her head back, stared at him in disbelief. "How do you know?"

"I drove them there myself."

She continued to stare. "But how —?"

"Toni called me."

She closed her eyes in relief. "God bless Toni."

"I went straight to the school and took them out of

class."

"They let you?"

Grant's mouth twisted. "Bethany Hammond and I are old friends."

Weak with relief, Janet let her full weight sag against him.

Grant kept her close with his left arm. He transferred his attention to Bart. "Okay," he said, his voice calm, though his tone was steely, "it's time to talk." He gestured toward the house. "We'll go inside."

Janet straightened away from him, disbelief flaring in her eyes. "What—? What are you doing?"

Did she think he was being too easy on Bart after the way he'd threatened and manhandled her?

"Have you lost your mind?"

Grant could appreciate her over-the-top response to his suggestion, but she'd soon understand he had a plan. He knew what he was doing. He squinted at the low-hanging clouds. "I don't know about you, but I'm as wet as I care to get."

"Oh." Janet pulled the collar of her jacket closer around her neck as if she'd only that moment realized rain was dripping off her wild bush of hair, soaking her collar and trickling down her neck. "Right." She took a step toward the house.

"Hey! Wait a minute." Bart grabbed at her arm to stop her. "Who is this guy?"

"Grant Brooks." Grant offered the answer. "And you are?"

"Bart O'Grady." Bart shifted his attention to Janet. "Look, I'm not interested in having a big conversation. You know what I want. Just give it to me and I'll leave."

Grant didn't know enough about Bart O'Grady to

predict his behavior, but he did know from long experience that the person who took charge of a situation had a good chance of maintaining the upper hand. "You want to know where the missing money is? We'll talk about it inside."

Janet seemed as unwilling as Bart to comply, but she led the way as they trooped to the house. Bart followed. Favoring his right leg, Grant noticed.

Inside, Janet shrugged out of her wet jacket and draped it over the back of a kitchen chair.

Bart hunched deeper into his rain-dampened windbreaker.

Grant took off his suit coat and casually tossed it on the granite counter. His tie already hung loose around his neck, the way it had been when Toni's panicked phone call galvanized him.

"Grant, you have to come quick," she'd begged. "I did a terrible thing. A guy from Sacramento came looking for Janet and I told him where she lived." She gulped a sob. "He said he was a friend and—"

Grant had cut her off right there because he knew without a doubt she was talking about Bart O'Grady, and that Janet and her boys were in grave danger. He'd raced out of the building to the parking lot, jumped into his vehicle and broken all speed limits, first to take the twins to their grandparents' house, then to reach Janet. He didn't care if he was fined for a dozen traffic violations or had to spend a week behind bars for evading an officer. Janet was in trouble. He had to get to her before this thug did. He hadn't quite made it...

Grant pulled out a chair and motioned for the other two to do the same. Amazingly, they both complied.

"Now," he said, resting his folded hands on the

table, "about the money."

Bart scowled at him. "I don't know who you are, but this is none of your business. This is strictly between me and Janet."

"It became my business when Janet asked me for advice."

Bart looked skeptical. "What kind of advice?"

"What to do with the money."

"The money isn't hers to do anything with. It belongs to me." Bart's delivery bordered on belligerence. "I demand to know where she and Marty hid it."

Grant wanted to plough his fist into Bart's ugly mug and shut him up, but he forced himself to stay calm. "That doesn't surprise me. There's a lot of it. More than six million at last tally." He leveled a hard look at Bart. "And you can stop blaming Janet. This was all your brother's doing. She came across the evidence by accident and did the right thing."

Bart thrust his big head forward. "The right thing was to give it to me." The words came out through tightly clenched teeth.

"Not in this case. But before we get into that, let me set your mind at ease, Bart. The money's safe. For the moment."

Grant leaned back in his chair as if this were an average, everyday conversation in his CEO's office at the bank. He was totally in the driver's seat. "I've been looking into your business, Bart, and so have a few of my colleagues. I'm a banker, by the way."

Bart made a movement that looked to Grant like something between a squirm and a wince. He also saw Bart check for the nearest exit.

"One of my colleagues is ex-FBI."

That bit of information had Bart scraping back his chair.

"It appears that you and your brother have been involved in some pretty sketchy dealings for a lot of years, and your investors have lodged complaints. Several want out."

Bart scowled. "The complaints are being addressed."

"I'm curious. You gave Janet this sob story about the company needing to liquidate its assets to avert bankruptcy? She believed you and relinquished her home and everything in it to you."

Bart nodded grudgingly.

"Yet my detective friend—that would be the ex-FBI—tells me you are now living in Janet's house."

Janet stared at Bart. "You weasel!" she exclaimed, and brought her fist down on the table with a thump strong enough to dislodge the cork coasters. They slid onto the Maplewood surface like a clumsily dealt hand of playing cards.

Grant wanted to grin, but he didn't. "And would that be the company Mercedes that's parked on the driveway outside?"

"This has nothing do to with the missing money."

Bart's bluster had little effect on Grant. "You've a right to be upset with your brother. He embezzled and hid the company's money, but the fact remains: The money itself was acquired illegally."

"Not all of it."

Grant could actually see Bart biting down on his tongue, as if he realized he'd just made what amounted to an admission of guilt. Grant pushed to his feet. "Sorry, Bart. No matter how you cut it, you're guilty of a whole whack of felonies, not the least of which was making repeated threats against Janet and her sons, and assaulting Janet just now."

Bart shoved his chair back with a clatter and leaped to his feet. "You can't prove that. You can't prove anything."

Grant took a step toward him. "That, my friend, is where you're wrong. The colleagues I mentioned have already referred this matter to the proper authorities who will be contacting you soon. My advice to you is to hurry home as fast as you can and do whatever you must to get your house in order. If you come clean about your business, it might help you stay outside of prison bars. Or not.

"Oh, by the way," he added, "the FBI will be happy to tell you where your brother stashed the money."

* * *

The front door slammed shut and for a moment, there was silence in the kitchen.

Janet struggled out of her chair, but her legs seemed too weak to hold her. She felt her body folding like an accordion.

Grant was around the table in a flash. He wrapped his arms around to hold her upright.

Her whole body was shaking. She buried her face in the sanctuary of his chest. "I was terrified, Grant. He saw the boys at the school."

Grant rubbed circles of comfort on her back. "Maybe so, but I don't think he ever meant to harm them. It was all a bluff, Janet, to scare you into talking."

Her tears were beginning to soak his shirt front. "He knew what they were wearing."

Grant pressed her even closer. "They're safe. No one's going to hurt them."

She sniffed noisily, hoping in a moment of rationality that she wasn't getting more than tears on his shirt. "Thank you for rescuing them."

Grant's voice, low and husky, rumbled in her ear. "Why wouldn't I? I love those boys like they were my own."

She knew it was true, and the fact made her guiltily aware of how deeply she had wounded him over the shoe episode. Sobs convulsed her. "I'm so sorry, Grant. I'm a horrible person. I don't deserve your help."

"Hush... There's not a thing about you that's horrible. You're wonderful."

The warmth of his breath caressing her temple made her shiver. She really should move away.

"Do you promise me Freddy and Teddy are safe—?"

"I promise."

Grant pressed his face into the soggy tangle of her hair and inhaled a somewhat shaky breath. That was when she realized that he was in no better control than she was. —Grant, who'd been the picture of confidence and composure through the whole exchange with Bart.

His vulnerability undid her. She lifted her teary face and cupped his cheek with her hand. The faintest emergence of beard pricked deliciously against her palm.

"You're shaking," she whispered, touched that he cared so deeply for her children.

Grant placed his hand over hers and moved it to his mouth. His lips were warm against her palm. His eyes, dark with remnants of the recent turbulence, searched hers. "Did he hurt you?"

Janet sniffed wetly and shook her head. "He scared me more than anything."

Grant released her hand and his fingertips traced the raised red imprint of Bart's hand on her cheek, then trailed down the column of her throat. His touch left a trail of fire in their wake. "You may have bruises."

"They'll go away," she whispered.

His palm very slowly moved down her neck and along the curve of her shoulder, then eased to her side and around to the back of her waist where his hands came together and pressed her closer still.

Somehow her own arms had found their way around Grant's neck and her fingertips were exploring the crispness of his hair. Standing there in his embrace, pressed against him, feeling his thudding heart matching hers beat for beat, there was nowhere else she wanted to be. In his arms was where she belonged. Where she longed to stay forever.

"I wanted to kill him."

His gruff confession brought a faint smile to Janet's lips. She looked up at him. "Really? You seemed so calm I thought you didn't care how it all turned out."

Grant pressed his forehead to hers. "Oh, I cared, all right. More than you know. It took every bit of self-control to keep my fist from plowing into his face."

She hiccupped a laugh. "That's what I was kinda hoping you'd do."

Grant's smile was rueful. "I've learned that you get a lot further with calm and reason than with belligerence. Are you terribly disappointed in me?"

"Never." Her fingers barely touched the pulse point in his neck. "You're my hero."

Grant's breath caught. His eyes dropped to her mouth, so close to his.

"Janet..." Her name came out as a needy groan.

The desire for him to kiss her was so strong Janet could hardly breathe. Her whole body felt weak with wanting.

Grant dipped his head. His lips were a mere inch away from hers. She could already feel their warmth.

Her fingers dove into the hair at the back of his head and she closed her eyes. Her senses swirled as she held her breath, waiting. Her lips throbbed, anticipating the magic touch of his mouth on hers.

But it never came.

Instead, she felt the chill of space between them as Grant dropped his arms and took a step backward.

She felt abandoned.

Color raced up her face.

She'd done it again.

Janet took her own backward step. "I'm sorry," she whispered through fingers pressed to trembling lips.

"No..." Grant's voice was hoarse and unsteady. "I'm the one who should be sorry."

Janet shook her head, unable to form appropriate words. Shame burned bright in her face. How could she have slipped so far from reality? Had she lost her mind? Most embarrassing was how hungry she'd been for his kiss. And how disappointed to miss it.

Equally regrettable was how easily she had forgotten about Christa. How easily she would have betrayed her own flesh and blood.

No way was Grant to blame. That lay squarely on her. He was merely responding to his God-given masculine instinct to protect a hurting female. To offer comfort and reassurance. Give her time to get a grip on her emotions. She'd probably imagined the almost kiss.

Thank God, he was a man of honor or things might have gone much differently.

Grant shuffled his feet. It was clear he wanted to say more, but instead he snagged his suit coat off the counter and bunched it under his arm. "I need to go." He hesitated. "You'll be okay?"

She'd never be okay.

Not ever.

But Grant didn't need to hear that.

"Yes." Her eyes held his for one brief, eloquent second. "Thank you."

She watched him turn and walk away. Through the mudroom. Out the backdoor. She listened until the sound of his vehicle faded in the distance.

Grant was gone.

Out of her life.

For good this time, and that was for the best. Because there was no other way.

She slumped on the nearest chair, cradled her head in her arms, and wept.

Chapter 19

"**Hello?** Janet?"

Janet poked her head out the main floor powder room door. "Yes, Mrs. Keeler?"

"I'm leaving now, but you know what to do."

"Dust the living room, polish the front windows and vacuum the entry." Janet ticked off the remaining tasks on her fingers.

Her client shook her head, sending her expensively-styled steel-gray hair swaying. "Who would think a half-dozen old women could make such a mess," she said. "They were only here for bridge and lunch. I can't for the life of me figure out how their fingerprints ended up all over my windows."

"It must be the view," Janet suggested with a smile. And indeed, the vista from the west-facing windows of the Keelers' stately Olympia home was stunning, with gardens below, the Capitol Building in the distance on the left, and the marina on Budd Inlet to the right. "It's lovely."

"Yes, it is," Mrs. Keeler agreed, "and I hope you'll feel free to have your lunch in the solarium. The view is even nicer from there. It's my favorite room."

Janet smiled her thanks. "I'll take my lunch break as soon as I've finished cleaning the powder room."

"And you'll make sure the doors are locked when you leave?"

"Absolutely."

Mrs. Keeler was a regular client of Ever Clean, the

housekeeping service for which Janet had been working for almost a month now. Wages were paid weekly, for which she was grateful. That, plus the free apartment she'd been able to score in exchange for custodial services in the building, provided a modest but predictable income.

The way the whole thing came about was nothing short of a miracle, she reflected not for the first time as she unpacked her simple lunch on the glass-topped solarium table a half hour later. It had been like an immediate answer to a desperate prayer.

"Thank you, Lord," she murmured aloud, both for the solution to her dilemma and the food she was about to eat.

After nearly forcing Grant to kiss her, she knew it was time to physically remove herself from his life. She'd known it long before, but the episode with Bart convinced her she couldn't delay a minute longer. Staying on at Pop's house was too risky. Everything there reminded her of Grant, and sooner or later he was bound to drop in for one reason or another, and the bald truth was, she didn't trust herself with him. Not given the way she felt about him and the rush of heat that continued to consume her every time she thought about the almost-kiss. So, when she spotted the apartment ad in the paper that very same day, she viewed it as a provision from God and checked into it immediately.

Fortunately, she was also able to work out a school bus arrangement so the twins could continue attending Ever Green Elementary. Not that they were happy about relocating. "We love Pop's house," they protested at least a dozen times a day.

She loved the house, too.

But that was beside the point.

Janet rolled a spoonful of Greek yogurt on her tongue and eased her feet onto the high ottoman that matched the cushioned chair in which she was basking in the pleasure of the moment.

These days, she was making a concerted effort to live in the moment. To appreciate and enjoy her blessings, however small, however brief. This definitely qualified as a blessing. What could be more pleasant than relaxing with good healthy food in front of a spectacular vista?

The Keelers' home was exactly the kind of place Christa wanted when she and Grant were married. Had they looked at any similar properties? Janet hoped so. It struck her as ironic that not so long ago she'd wondered why her sister and Grant didn't choose to live in Pop's house. Now her heart rejected the idea absolutely, but she didn't want to explore the reason why.

Janet licked the last smear of yogurt off the spoon and tucked it into a resealable plastic bag to take home with her. Truth be told, she didn't want to think about any of that. Not the wedding, or where they'd live. Most of all, she didn't want to think about Grant, because every time she did, her heart ached and her spirit became unspeakably sad.

Her heart was being stupidly slow at accepting that Grant was not, could not, would not ever be hers. She'd lost count of the times she'd given her misplaced love to God and prayed, *"Father, be Enough for me... Loving Grant isn't right, but I can't seem to help myself. Please give me Your strength. You say in Your Word You'll be husband to the widow and father to the fatherless. I ask that You'll be that for me and my boys. Please, Father...be Enough."*

As often as she prayed that prayer, God seemed to comfort her with the thought that, though her love might be misplaced, it was not a mistake. Just knowing Grant Brooks had made her a better person. And what a wonderful male role model he was for her boys. Had been. Would still be, if she could successfully rein in her feelings.

She had determined, with God's help, to live beyond how she felt for Grant. No one else need ever know. She would live a fruitful, independent life. But one thing was for sure. There could be no repeats of that last emotionally charged encounter.

Janet leaned her head against the overstuffed chair cushion and bit into a crisp, red-skinned apple. Coming back to Ever Green had seriously complicated her life, but more and more she was realizing that returning was not a mistake. She was working out her goal of building a good and healthy life for her boys. She now lived independently, had a job and a place of her own. She'd told her parents everything, begged their forgiveness for her actions in the past, and was now well on the way to building an honest and loving relationship with them. And now that Bart and his threats were out of the picture, she was experiencing a freedom and sense of security that she hadn't felt in years.

Life was good.

Her biggest problem at the moment was the impending wedding. In a matter of days now, the man her heart cherished would be forever joined before God and man to not just anyone, but to her sister. And given the man of integrity she knew Grant to be, the commitment he made would be for life. Would she be able to dredge up the composure to walk down the aisle, stand beside her sister — almost within touching distance of Grant — and watch him pledge himself to another?

Only with God's help...

"I'm farmished," Freddy declared as he slouched out of his backpack and hooked his jacket on the low hanger she'd installed inside the apartment's hall closet.

Janet bit down on the inside of her cheek. "Farmished? Really? Then it's probably a good thing I have a snack ready for you."

The twins made a beeline for the table in the tiny dining nook where Janet had already laid out glasses of milk and a plate of crackers, cheese and fruit. Teddy slid onto a chair, lifted his glass. "Cheers!" he crowed.

Freddy responded in kind and the pair touched glass rims and chorused: "We clink and then we drink."

Where did they learn these things?

The ring of the telephone prevented Janet from inquiring.

It was her mother.

Verna didn't waste time with small talk. "You need to get out here right away," she said.

The blunt directive marched a whole squadron of goose bumps up Janet's arms. "What's happened? Is it Dad?"

Verna's voice was grim. "Your father's fine. He's out talking business with some fellow from Seattle."

"What, then?"

Her mother drew a sharp, impatient breath. "Just come."

It was not a polite suggestion.

"Okay... We'll be there as soon as we can." A sudden

thought made Janet hesitate. "This isn't some...family pow-wow, is it?" *Translation: Grant isn't going to be there, is he?* Because if he was, she'd be heading in the opposite direction.

"Janet," Verna hissed, "just get over here."

Twenty-five minutes later Janet turned the Jeep Grand Cherokee into the lane leading up to Ever Green Acres. Christa was there, she noted, spotting her sister's little white Miata at the end of the drive. That seemed unusual this early in the afternoon until Janet remembered that Christa had ended her job at the library to concentrate fully on the wedding.

The Jeep had scarcely rolled to a stop before Verna was tapping on the driver side window.

Janet obligingly lowered it.

"Christa doesn't know I called you," Verna hissed. "Can you pretend you just happened by?"

"O – kay."

The twins followed their usual routine of leaping out of the Jeep and doing a marathon sprint around the yard. When they completed the circuit, Janet knew they would head for their grandmother's kitchen expecting treats.

Janet trailed her mother into the house. Something must have happened to Christa. Was she sick? Had she had an accident?

Apparently not. Christa was looking perfectly healthy — as much as Janet could see of her sister as Christa darted around the kitchen, snatching cocoa from one cupboard, vanilla from another, dumping random amounts of each into a big bowl and furiously beating the contents.

She peeked over Christa's shoulder. "What's

happening here?"

"Brownies." Christa's voice was bright.

Too bright.

"The boys will like that."

Brownies had always been Christa's favorite comfort food from the time she was a little girl. Whenever a friend let her down, or she did poorly in a test, or some other disappointment befell her, Christa had drowned her sorrows in brownies.

"So what's up?"

Christa's head jerked around. "Why do you ask?"

Could that possibly be red eyeliner? Or had her sister been crying?

"No reason. You seem upset about something."

"Upset—? Why would I be upset?"

Janet waved an apologetic hand. "Sorry, poor choice of word. Make that agitated."

"I'm perfectly fine." Christa angled the mixing bowl over a square cake pan and scraped the chocolaty batter into it—with more vigor than necessary, to Janet's mind.

Yup, something was definitely wrong.

Christa opened the oven, shoved the pan inside and set the timer. Then she crossed to the sink to rinse the utensils she'd used and stack them in the dishwasher, all with enough noise to preclude any hope of conversation.

"How was your day?" Janet ventured when at last the dishwasher door was closed and relative quiet reigned.

"My day?" Christa looked like she might actually have given an answer had not the back door burst open at that precise moment and the twins exploded into the kitchen.

"Shoes," Janet reminded them, swallowing her

frustration at the interruption.

Teddy backtracked to the mudroom, kicked off his light-up runners, and was back in a jiffy. "What smells so yummy?"

Christa twisted away from the counter and enclosed her nephews in a group hug. "Brownies. I made them just for the two of you."

Sure you did, Janet thought. *You didn't even know we were coming...*

"When can we have some?"

"Won't be long."

Had she ever seen Christa this artificially animated?

"In the meantime, I need your help with something very important."

The twins were eager, as always, to lend a helping hand. "What do we have to do?"

"It's a kind of game," Christa told them, folding herself to six-year-old size so she could look Freddy and Teddy in the eye. "You two stay here. I'll be right back."

She disappeared down the hall and returned a few minutes later with a large map of the world which she spread out on the kitchen table.

The boys looked doubtful; Janet was frankly baffled.

"What kind of game can we play with that?" Freddy wondered.

"Wait and see." Christa whipped a silk scarf from the pocket of her designer jeans. "This will be our blindfold. Who wants to go first?"

"I do," the twins chorused.

Christa put her hand on Freddy's shoulder. "You can go first." She quickly tied the scarf around his head and made sure his eyes were covered. "Now," she announced, "I'm going to give you a pin." She produced a large-headed poster pin and put it in the boy's hand.

"What do I do with it?"

Janet wondered the same thing.

"You're going to stick it in the map. Anywhere you want," Christa informed him.

Freddy turned his sandy head toward the sound of her voice. "Anywhere?"

"Anywhere."

Freddy approached the table, waved his arm in an elaborate configuration, and brought the pin down as far as his six-year-old arm could reach, near the top. He pulled off the silk scarf. "Did I do good?"

"Hmmm..." Christa pinched her lips together. "You've put me on Baffin Island. I think I'm going to need a second opinion. You ready, Teddy?"

Teddy giggled. "Ready Teddy....that rhymes." He tried it again, several times, while Christa secured the blindfold in place.

Janet's frown deepened. She had no idea what her sister was up to, but something deep inside said it wasn't anything good.

Teddy's pin landed in the blue Atlantic.

"Let me see." Christa leaned closer. "Grand Bahama Island. Teddy, my darling, you did good. I like it. You win."

Teddy tore off the scarf. "What did I win?"

"The first brownie," Christa declared and rushed to the oven where the timer had begun emitting an annoying buzz. She pulled out the pan and placed it on the counter. "And you, Freddy, will get the second one." She carefully cut and lifted out a generous slice of steaming brownie for each plate. "These are hot. How about I put some ice cream on top to cool them off?"

Without waiting for a response, she hauled a tub of ice cream from the freezer and added a double scoop to first one, then the other of the brownie plates. She set the dessert plates on top of the map and the twins immediately tucked into the hot/cold treat.

Only then did Christa flicker a glance at her mother and Janet. "Do you want brownies, too?"

Both women shook their heads.

Janet sauntered up beside her. "Okay, time's up, Chris... What this all about?"

"What? The map?"

The map, the manufactured cheer, the hyperactivity... Janet gave a slow, watchful nod.

"Your son just picked my holiday destination."

Teddy proudly bumped a thumb against his chest. "That son was me, Mommy," he declared and shoveled another forkful of cream-drenched brownie into his mouth. "Can Freddy and me have another brownie when we're done this?" he inquired.

"Your holiday destination?" Janet stared at her sister. "Don't you mean your honeymoon destination?"

It was an odd way to pick a honeymoon venue, especially at this late date. Besides, wasn't that Grant's job? Other than offering his credit card for unlimited usage, she'd been given to understand that arranging the honeymoon destination was the one wedding task Christa had entrusted to him.

Christa used her finger to capture a trail of brownie crumbs on the counter. "There is no honeymoon. I'm going alone."

Verna gasped and exchanged a see-I-told-you-something-was-going-on look with Janet.

"More brownies, Mommy?"

Janet grabbed the knife, made an absent-minded slice across the width of the baking pan, quickly divided the strip in two and dispensed half onto each plate—all without taking her eyes off her sister.

The twins couldn't believe their good fortune. They eyed the oversized brownies with amazement, then silently high-fived each other across the table. Wisely, they refrained from asking for more ice cream.

Janet crossed her arms and leaned against the table. "Okay. What's going on?"

Christa brushed her white-blond bangs off her forehead and raised one perfect eyebrow. "The wedding's off."

Janet tapped her palm against her ear. "I thought I just heard you say the wedding's off."

"You heard right."

"What on earth are you talking about?"

"Is it so difficult to understand, Janet? My wedding's off, I returned the wedding dress, and now I'm taking myself on a holiday to—" she leaned over to consult the world map "—to Grand Bahama Island. What more would you like to know?"

Janet huffed out an exasperated breath. "Just about everything! For starters, since when is the wedding off?"

"Since yesterday."

Scorching gastric reflux headed upward in Janet's throat. "Whose idea was that?"

Christa lifted both hands, palms up. "Does it matter?"

The way her conscience was prickling? Yes, it mattered a great deal. "I'm just curious."

Christa avoided her eyes. "It was...a mutual decision."

Janet didn't believe that for a minute. Grant had broken the engagement. She was sure of it. Was it because of the near-kiss? She hoped not, because that wonderful, awful moment of betrayal wasn't his fault. It was totally hers. Or had Grant called off the wedding because he was afraid she'd continue to throw herself at him, that eventually her advances would be so aggressive and impossible to resist that it would break up his marriage?

Well, he was wrong. She would never, ever put him in that position again. She had learned her lesson. She was moving on.

She crossed to Christa's side and put an arm around her older sister's shoulders. "Come on, Chris. If you and Grant had a disagreement, you'll get past it. It's a normal part of pre-wedding jitters."

...As if she knew what was normal pre-, post-, or in the middle of a wedding. Or in a marriage, for that matter. But her mother would know. Janet looked at Verna for support. "Isn't that right, Mom?"

Verna had been silent, with her hand pressed to her mouth, throughout the whole exchange. Now she shook her head helplessly, apparently still struggling to fathom what this unexpected bombshell meant.

Thanks for the help, Mom...

Janet gave Christa's arm a little squeeze. "The arrangements are all made. People are coming. Mom and Dad will be so disappointed."

"They'll get over it."

For all her bold words, Janet could see Christa's bravado was fading. She heard the pain in her sister's voice. Very gently, she pressed her cheek to Christa's. "I know Mom and Dad will get over it, hon, but will you?"

Christa pulled away and drew a noisy breath. "It's only my pride that's hurt." She flashed a practiced smile that revealed her perfectly white teeth. "Now, if you'll excuse me, I have a flight to book."

Chapter 20

Janet perched nervously on the edge of the apartment's brown tweed sofa and dialed the number for Grant's bank. It was Saturday, but the bank was open Saturdays so there was a slim chance that Grant might be there. She certainly hoped so, because she really didn't look forward to the prospect of having to call his cell phone. That seemed too intimate, somehow. Too personal...

But she did need to get in touch with him.

And soon.

Things had happened quickly following Christa's shocking announcement yesterday, so fast that Janet could hardly keep her thoughts straight. Against all odds, it seemed, Christa had been able to arrange for a flight out of SeaTac Airport the very next day — today, in fact — and thanks to trusty Google, had found a luxurious-sounding beach-front hotel in Freeport, Bahamas, where she had booked herself a room for two weeks.

Janet offered to drive her to the airport, but Christa declined. She'd drive herself, she insisted. That way it wouldn't matter to anyone when she returned.

Was there a hidden message in there somewhere...?

"Ever Green Financial. How may I direct your call?"

Janet's hand tightened on the phone. "Is Mr. Brooks in?"

"I don't believe so, ma'am, but I'll connect you with his secretary."

Janet pictured the gray-haired woman she'd met on

her previous visit to the bank, the day she'd come clean about finding the money in Pop's kitchen. She heaved a weary sigh. A veritable torrent of ugly river water had churned beneath the bridge since that particular encounter.

"Mr. Brooks' office."

"Good morning." Janet cleared her throat. "Would Grant— I mean, would Mr. Brooks be in?"

"I'm sorry, but Mr. Brooks is away. He won't be back in his office until the fifth of January."

Of course. Why hadn't she thought of that? Like Christa, Grant would be taking off time for the wedding and the honeymoon.

"Is there anyone else who can help you?"

"No. Thank you."

"All right, then," the secretary said. "Have a nice day."

"No! Wait!" Janet's fingers clamped tighter on the phone. "Is there a number where I can reach him?"

The secretary's tone cooled. "I can't give you that information, miss."

No, of course you can't...

"Right. Thanks. Sorry to bother you."

Janet ended the call and slumped against the worn cushions. It looked like his cell phone was her only option.

She rose and paced the small living room, ending up by the window that overlooked a shabby courtyard made even more uninviting by the winter rains. She was glad the boys were at her parents' house where they would spend the night. At least *they* were having a good time.

Janet expelled a great huffy breath. She blamed

Christa for all this nervousness and uncertainty. Oh, not because the wedding was cancelled and Christa had taken herself off to a sunny Caribbean island. What Janet was struggling with was the task Christa had forced upon her at the last moment.

She'd stayed at the farm to help Christa pack, and just as Janet was preparing to leave, Christa had shoved her wedding journal at her.

"Give this to Grant," she said, her features stony. "He called off the wedding, the least he can do is cancel the arrangements."

So calling off the wedding *was* Grant's doing. Just as Janet suspected. That opened a whole new world of complications, not the least was that she would be forced to see him again face-to-face.

And she really wasn't ready to do that.

The mental picture of throwing herself into his arms, clinging to him, practically begging him to make love to her, was still too vivid and humiliatingly painful. She couldn't face Grant. Couldn't stand to know his opinion of her after such a shameless display.

But did she have a choice? Getting the wedding book to him wasn't something for a later date, when her shame and embarrassment had faded to an acceptable level. The fact was, there were only ten days left before the wedding was scheduled to take place and cancellations had to be made immediately. Even so, Grant was going to incur hefty financial penalties for backing out of some arrangements on such short notice.

Janet pressed her fingers to her pulsing temples. She had to think rationally. Did she have the nerve to call Grant on his cell phone? A conversation with him would be unbearably awkward. It would be so much easier just to leave a quick message. Or simply deliver the book to his door.

Maybe stick it in his mailbox and then run like a coward...

That was the ticket.

Only problem was, she didn't know exactly where Grant lived. She knew he had a condo somewhere, but the telephone directory offered only the landline number, not the address.

She sighed and picked up the phone again. Grant's cell number was programmed in. She pressed the appropriate key and tried to ignore the accelerated thumping of her heart. She waited, breath tight, mentally rehearsing the words she'd say.

One ring...

Two rings...

A voice cut in. "We're sorry, the customer you are trying to reach is unavailable. Please try again later."

Relief oozed from her pores like sweat, but it was quickly followed by cold, steely dread at the realization that only one option remained. She would have to deliver the wedding book to Grant's condo.

Wherever that was.

Her mother might know.

Janet scooped up her purse and the wedding book and headed out to the Jeep. She'd stop by the farm, make sure the boys weren't driving her parents crazy, maybe have lunch with them and get the information she needed from her mother — then deliver herself to the guillotine.

Bone-chilling rain kept the windshield wipers busy as Janet headed toward Ever Green Acres. A convulsive shiver while she waited for the heater to warm the interior brought a pang of envy for the sunny Caribbean climes toward which Christa was winging. Janet checked her watch. Factoring in the time differential between Washington State and the Bahamas, she calculated that Christa would be stepping off the plane in exactly one and a half hours. It would be early evening in Freeport. Maybe Christa would go for a walk on the beach. That's what *she* would do if she was in Christa's sandals.

But she wasn't. She was here, in the rain, trying to deal with the complications that Christa had left behind, the complications *she* herself had created.

When The Tireman sculpture's glistening black tire-head appeared above the trees, Janet automatically checked the gas tank. It could use a top-up, she decided. Besides, she hadn't seen Toni in a while. Maybe a quick visit with her friend was just the psychological boost she needed. Heaven knew she was in no hurry to complete her assignment despite its urgency.

"I got my dress for the wedding," Toni announced almost the moment Janet walked through the door. "It's fancier than what I usually buy, but I thought: What the heck? I've known Christa forever, and Grant is a good friend. The dress is ruby red. It looks great on. I'll wear my Grandma Cirelli's ruby pendant and earrings. She brought them from Italy when she and Grandpa were newlyweds. They're family heirlooms."

Janet had never heard Toni chatter like this before. She could only hope there would be some other significant event in Toni's future where she could wear this extra-special dress...

"There isn't going to be a wedding."

Toni's jaw dropped. She blinked. And blinked again.

"The wedding's off. They cancelled it. By mutual agreement." It seemed fairer to say it that way.

"Why?"

Janet gave an expressive shrug. "Your guess is as good as mine."

Not true...

"I can't believe it. How is Christa?"

"She left this morning for the Bahamas."

Toni's jaw fell even further. "What about Grant?"

"Haven't seen him. But I need to. Christa left it to him to cancel the arrangements. She has everything documented in a kind of journal that I need to get to him. But he's taken a month of vacation and I don't know where he is."

"I do." Toni was still looking stunned by the news. "He's at Pop's house."

"Pop's house?"

"Yup." Toni stepped behind the counter to print out Janet's fuel bill. "He stopped in yesterday for gas. He looks terrible."

* * *

Grant shoved his fingertips into the back pockets of his jeans and stared out the kitchen window. Rain slanted down from the heavily overcast sky, effectively veiling his view of the backyard. The backyard in which he'd spent so many joyful hours over the past weeks and months getting it back into shape. Making it beautiful again.

For Janet.

He turned away from the window and wandered aimlessly toward the living room where a fire crackled in the fireplace. It had taken the chill out of the room, but it wasn't doing a thing to diminish the chill inside of him.

After a week of personal neglect, he'd finally forced himself to take a shower this morning and shave off a week's worth of beard. It was about time; his appearance hadn't been pretty. The curl of Christa's lip yesterday said it all. Or maybe her distaste had more to do with her opinion of him for putting an end to her carefully-orchestrated plans and dreams.

The last thing he wanted to do was hurt Christa, but he'd known for a while, almost from the moment Janet O'Grady came to town, that he would hurt Christa more by marrying her than by breaking their engagement. At the same time, he was acutely aware she would suffer humiliation from being left at the altar. But every time he was with Janet, every time he looked at her— No, every time he even thought about her, he felt disloyal. And the fact that she was Christa's sister only made the disconnect more profound.

He'd prayed about it long and hard, even gone into a sort of seclusion here at Pop's house to do it. Two days ago, he'd finally known for certain what he had to do.

Grant wandered back to the kitchen and slumped onto one of the wooden chairs. He didn't like himself much for what he'd done to Christa, but in time, he hoped, she'd come to accept that ending their relationship had been merciful on his part. Christa was too fine a woman to be stuck for life with a guy who didn't love her.

Not that he'd really known anything about love until he met Janet.

He missed Janet.

He ached for her.

Longed to be with her.

Had thought of nothing else for days. For weeks. For months, if the truth be told. But only now could he think about her without being inundated by a tsunami of guilt.

A lot of help that was when she'd deliberately removed herself from all contact with him. That should probably tell him volumes.

Grant parked his elbows on the table and propped his forehead on bunched fists. He felt like a battle-weary soldier. He'd been waging war with himself for so long now that he hardly knew what was right. Yes he was free, but he didn't know if he could face Janet. She probably hated him for what he'd done to her sister. But even if she never spoke to him again, at least he had the satisfaction of knowing he'd done the right thing by Christa.

He leaned back in the chair and looked around the kitchen, still neat and orderly, the way Janet had left it.

Funny... Before Janet, whenever he came to this house, it was his grandparents he missed. He recalled sitting across the table from Pop having a cup of that awful instant coffee Pop liked to make. Now all he could picture was Janet, plying him with fresh apple pie and good brewed coffee. And her boys, Freddy and Teddy, bursting into the house, eyes dancing, energy fairly spewing from their pores, begging him to play with them. How he loved those two.

In time, would Janet forgive him—? He had to believe she would. Had to hang onto that hope. He was willing to wait no matter how long it took, because he couldn't imagine giving her up forever.

"Enough, Brooks," he growled aloud. "Get a grip. You're a basket case."

For his own sanity's sake, he needed to shift his thinking to something less devastating. Maybe he should make himself a cup of Pop's good ol' instant coffee.

He got up, crossed to the stove, and reached for his grandmother's whistling tea kettle that hadn't whistled since the day he'd inadvertently dropped it on the tile floor and the special lid that produced the whistle broke off. You could still boil water in it, but without the lid, the kettle was incapable of fulfilling its full potential.

Sort of like him, Grant reflected as he filled the kettle with water and put it on the burner. For a long time he'd been feeling less than complete, less than fulfilled. Crippled by some missing element in his life, the element that kept him feeling like he was falling short. Only recently had he come to identify the element he longed for to make him complete.

It was a wife and family.

Not just any convenient wife, or simply a beautiful companion, but one who loved him as deeply and wholeheartedly as he loved her. He wanted a woman to have and to hold as his wife. He wanted to be a father, too. He wanted to have children with his wife, wanted to pour his life into them. To be part of a family that was devoted to one another.

He probably needed to revise all that. The real truth was: The piece missing from his life was Janet. She was the one he wanted to have and to hold as his wife. He wanted her boys to be his children. He wanted to marry Janet and have other children with her.

Unfortunately, the way things were going, it didn't look as if that particular missing piece was meant to fall into place for him. He wished it were different. He wished he could get in his car, drive over to the apartment where he knew Janet and her boys were living and tell her how he felt about her. But given what he'd done to her sister, he was probably the last person she wanted to see.

By the time steam jetted upward from the kettle spout, Grant realized he wasn't interested in coffee anymore.

In fact, he wasn't interested in much of anything.

* * *

Rain was coming down hard when Janet parked the Jeep beside Grant's gold SUV. Her stomach was queasy with nervousness.

She shut off the motor and sat for a moment to gather her composure. On the short drive over from The Tireman, she'd rehearsed what she would say when she finally came face-to-face with Grant. Now she couldn't recall a word of it.

She lifted the wedding book from the seat and tucked it inside her jacket. If she had any luck at all, she would simply hand it to him and leave. That would be easiest on both of them. Grant was smart; he'd figure out what he had to do.

She slid out of the Jeep, made a quick dash to the back door and pressed the doorbell.

Grant didn't answer, but she could see lights on in the kitchen.

She pressed the doorbell again.

After what seemed an eternity, the door opened. Grant stood in the doorway.

His hair was longer than she'd ever seen it and looked like he'd groomed it with a garden rake. Half-moon shadows weighted the skin beneath his eyes, but he still looked wonderful.

"Janet?" His voice was gruff with surprise. His eyes roamed her face as if memorizing it.

"Toni—" Her voice cracked and she tried again. "Toni said you were here. I came to give you this." She pulled Christa's wedding book from the protection of her jacket and pushed it into his hands.

Grant didn't look at the book, didn't say anything. He just kept looking at her.

When his eyes did leave her face, they shifted to where the rain was pelting down behind her, splashing onto the flagstone landing and bouncing onto her canvas shoes and the hems of her jeans. He opened the door wider. "Come inside."

Janet stepped into the mudroom and was immediately swaddled in familiarity. Her mind flickered from memory to memory of the work she'd done eliminating the clutter in Pop's house, and the satisfaction she'd found in restoring its gracious beauty. She remembered the laughter she and Grant had shared those times he'd come to haul away the recyclables. What about the day the washer hose broke and the mudroom became a slippery lake? What followed was her first experience in Grant's arms. The recollection of that brought a rush of color to her cheeks, followed hard by guilt and a sense of disloyalty to her sister.

That's where all this mess they were in had started...

The thump of the wedding book being tossed onto the washer brought her back to the present.

Janet frowned, picked it up, and handed it back to Grant. "Christa asked me to give this to you." She spared him the word-for-word version of her sister's directive.

Once again, as if the wedding journal was the least of his concerns, Grant deposited it on the washer. "How *is* Christa?"

Janet gave him a sideways look that she hoped conveyed her disapproval of how he'd treated her sister. But she couldn't stop her heart from curling with warmth at the compassion in his voice. "She left this morning for the Bahamas."

Grant arched an eyebrow.

"It's a long story."

Why was she telling him that? Grant knew the story better than she did.

"I'm mad at you for cancelling the wedding."

"You are?"

No, not really. But it seemed the right thing to say. For her sister's sake, at least. "It wasn't very fair to Christa."

Grant's gray-green stormy-sea eyes bored into hers. "Trust me, Janet. It was the only right thing to do."

"How can you say that?" Did he think dumping Christa just days before her wedding wouldn't be hurtful and deeply humiliating?

"Christa will get over it." The words sounded harsh, until he added, "But I couldn't marry her, Janet. I don't love her."

Janet tilted her chin. "Well, your timing stinks. Too bad you didn't figure that out a whole lot sooner."

Grant raked his fingers through his hair. "I understand you're upset with me for Christa's sake, but believe me when I say it's for the best." He hesitated, as if unsure he should say more, then added, "I didn't do it sooner because it was only recently that I discovered what it is to genuinely and completely love a woman."

Color stained his cheeks and he shifted his stance. She'd never seen him this uncertain. It was rather endearing.

He cleared his throat and gestured awkwardly with his hand. "Look, the mudroom is no place to have this conversation. Take off your jacket and come in where it's warm. Would you like some hot cocoa? The water's already hot."

Should she stay, or should she leave? She'd already done what she came to do. Did she want to stay and parse his cryptic remarks, hear what else he had to say on the subject of love?

Something inside of her shouted a resounding, yes!

"Hot cocoa would be nice."

Grant headed for the kitchen and Janet shrugged out of her rain-dampened jacket. From habit, she hung it on the last peg on the coat rack. After placing her sodden shoes near the heat register, she followed him into the kitchen.

Everything in the kitchen looked exactly as she'd left it. "How long have you been here?"

Grant was in the pantry. Probably searching for the hot cocoa mix.

"Second shelf, left side."

"What—? Oh, right. Here it is. Thanks. What did you say?"

"I asked how long you've been here."

Grant placed the cocoa mix tin on the counter, pulled a pair of tall ceramic mugs from the cupboard and dug in the cutlery drawer for a spoon. "Since you left."

"Really?" She had no idea what to do with that bit of information, and no idea how to respond. She chose the safest route and escaped to the living room. It was her favorite room in Pop's house, made all the more inviting by the fire that was crackling in the fireplace.

"Where would you like to have your chocolate?" Grant called from the kitchen a few minutes later.

"In here?"

"Good choice."

He appeared in the arched doorway, carefully transporting two steaming mugs, each with an island of half-melted mini-marshmallows bobbing on the surface.

Janet relieved him of one mug and chose a seat on the sofa facing the hearth. When Grant settled beside her, she scooted to the far end. She'd expected him to take one of the wing chairs, establishing some distance between them.

"Where are the boys?"

"At the farm."

"How are they?"

"They're good."

Grant took a sip of his cocoa. "I miss those little guys." There was a wistful note in his voice so genuine it made her eyes prickle.

"They miss you, too." She was past the point of wanting to cover things up, avoiding the truth. "They tell me at least once a day how much they dislike living in the apartment. They didn't want to leave Pop's house."

Grant set his mug on the inlaid wooden bench that could be either coffee table or hassock, whichever the occasion demanded.

"Why did you leave?"

Chapter 21

Janet's mug clattered as she set it on the bench beside his. He wanted to know why she'd left Pop's house? "You want the truth?"

"Of course."

"It could be embarrassing..."

"I can handle embarrassing."

But could she?

Janet fixed her eyes on the fire so she wouldn't have to meet his searching gaze. So she wouldn't be tempted to fudge the truth, even if it might spare her embarrassment.

"I didn't feel I had much choice after the way I threw myself at you that day with Bart."

"What are you talking about?"

She dared a quick, disbelieving glance at him. "Come on, Grant. I all but begged you to make love to me. I knew I had to leave. I was afraid if I stayed here and you came back to the house—which you probably would have, sooner or later—the same thing might happen again. I refused to put you in that position."

To her shock and surprise, Grant threw back his head and laughed. His eyebrows reached for the boyish cowlick tumbling on his forehead. "*That* was your reason?"

Her nod was uncertain. "Why are you laughing?"

"Because it's so ironic. All this time I thought it was on me. I felt like a jerk because all I wanted to do that day was scoop you up in my arms and run for the hills.

After I'd kissed you senseless, of course. I was sure you could somehow read all that and were appalled, thinking I was hitting on you when I was just weeks away from marrying your sister."

That's what he'd thought? "You worried I thought you were hitting on me?"

Grant's forehead creased in a regretful frown. "I hate to phrase it that way. It sounds so cheap, and nothing at all like the feelings I have for you."

Wait a minute... He had feelings for her? Her heart did a giddy cartwheel at the possibility.

Her pulse rate shot even higher when he slid his arm along the back of the sofa and edged closer. "Surely you know, Janet... When I said I only recently discovered what it is to genuinely love a woman, I was talking about you. You're that woman."

Janet tipped her head back. Closed her eyes, savored his admission. Drew the words deep into her soul, absorbing what it meant. For her. For them.

Grant loved her? How was it possible?

She had to be sure she'd heard right. "Until two days ago, you were going to marry my sister."

Grant took a quick sip of chocolate, as if he needed the moment to frame his words.

"Christa and I have known each other for a long time, Janet. We had a comfortable relationship. Christa actually asked me out first. She needed a date for a social event. Later, I called her for the same reason. For all the time we were together, I admit — shallow as it sounds — I was proud to be seen with Christa on my arm."

Understandable. Christa had always been an attention magnet.

"But love didn't factor in for either of us. Our

relationship was just...convenient."

—Which was basically what Christa had said. Except that Christa also admitted to being fond of Grant's bank account.

"Then Christa started talking about marriage, and I guess I didn't discourage her. I always wanted a marriage like Pop and Gram had, but since I hadn't met any woman who made me feel the way Pop did about Gram, I figured that kind of love must only happened to a fortunate few and I wasn't one of them."

He spiraled one of her rain-dampened curls around his finger and gave it the gentlest of tugs, sending a ripple of exquisite sensation all the way down to her toes. "But everything changed when you blew into town. It didn't take long for me to recognize that I couldn't settle for anything less than marriage to a woman I loved with all my heart."

"I hope you let Christa down gently," she said after a long moment. "Did you tell her you were in...l-love with me?" The word, strange and still hard to believe, stumbled on her tongue.

Grant snagged her hand and meshed his fingers with hers. "I didn't. I felt it would be too hurtful." He said it almost apologetically. "Most important, I didn't want her blaming you."

Her heart swelled at his decency.

"I simply told Christa the truth, that it wasn't fair for us to marry when I don't love her as she deserves to be loved. I told her she deserves a husband who thinks the world of her. A man who loves her more than life itself and who can't imagine living another day without her."

Was that how Grant felt about her?

"I think Christa was more relieved than she let on,"

he added. "It's her pride that will take the biggest hit. I do feel bad about that."

"Are you absolutely sure about loving me, Grant? We've only known each other a few months."

A look of alarm froze his features. "Are you saying you don't feel the same way I do?"

"I'm not saying that at all. I'm just questioning—" *Whether I'm good enough for you?* "—whether it's possible to fall in love this quickly. How can you be sure I'm the woman for you?"

Relief softened his countenance. His hands cupped her shoulders and turned her toward him. His wonderful stormy sea eyes blazed with emotion.

"How do I know you're the woman for me? Because I'm only really alive when you're around. I love being with you. I think about you all the time. The most wonderful moments of my life have been when you were in my arms. I've waited all my life for you, my love. I know in my heart you're God's precious gift to me, to have and to hold. There will never be anyone else."

The wave of warmth sweeping over her had nothing to do with the dancing hearth fire. "I feel the same way, Grant" she whispered. "I know for a fact I'm truly in love for the first time."

Grant's laugh was exultant. He scooped her into his lap and bent to press a line of kisses along the soft flesh beneath her ear. The pleasure of it was almost painful, but Janet ached for him to give her the kind of kiss she'd dreamed about almost since the first day they met. She took his face in her hands and redirected his mouth to hers.

"Mmm..." he murmured against her lips. "You taste like chocolate. And marshmallows. I love chocolate and marshmallows."

"I'll keep that in mind." She loved the teasing nibbles, but a woman could only wait so long... "Kiss me properly," she whispered.

And Grant willingly obliged.

Long moments later, with her lips tingling from their kisses, Janet leaned back in Grant's arms and studied him with adoring eyes. Her fingers traced his jaw, and then brushed over his lips which were curved in a sensuous smile meant only for her. She smoothed his dark eyebrows and investigated the hump on his nose.

"How did you get this?"

The lines at the corners of his eyes crinkled. "It's an old football injury."

"In college?" There was so much she didn't know about Grant. So much she was eager to learn and would spend the rest of her life doing so.

"Nope. In kindergarten."

She swatted him with her hand. "Tell me the truth. How did it happen?"

Grant captured her hand and held it against his chest. "That's the truth. We were playing football in kindergarten and Johnny Smallman tackled me. I fell and smashed my nose against a rock. My mother was furious with Johnny for ruining my good looks."

"You poor boy." She planted a kiss of sympathy on the bump. "And your mother was wrong. It made you more handsome than ever."

Chuckling, Grant tucked her head into the curve of his neck. "So," he said, "what are we going to do about this?"

Janet shook her head. She was happy right where

she was, wrapped in his arms, reveling in the knowledge that the man she loved so completely felt the same love for her. She didn't want to think about complicated details. Not right now, anyway.

A rumble of amusement beneath her ear made her lift her head. "What's funny?"

"You should probably know I had a call from the twins about a week ago."

"Really—?"

"Oh yeah... Proposing marriage."

Janet pushed away, her mouth a perfect O of disbelief. "You're joking."

"No joke. As I recall, the conversation went something like this: 'Will you marry us, Uncle Grant? Mommy likes you a lot and we could all live together at Pop's house.'"

She shook her head and snickered. "What did you tell them?"

"I told them I'd like that very much."

Grant closed her mouth with a gentle finger under her chin. "I said yes, Janet, because I realized what they were proposing was exactly what I wanted, more than anything else in the world. That's when I knew it would be morally wrong for me to marry Christa. Especially when I couldn't imagine living the rest of my life without the three of you in it."

He grasped both her hands in his. "Please say you'll marry me, Janet."

"I— You—" Janet shook her head in bewilderment. What had just happened? An hour or so ago she'd hesitated to face him. Now... "I don't know what to say."

"Say yes."

Grant loved her. He wanted to marry her. She loved

him, too, but never once had she ever believed becoming his wife was a possibility.

Janet closed her eyes. "Maybe you'd better pinch me," she said. "I can't believe this is real. Surely I must be dreaming."

Grant pressed a sweet kiss to her lips. "Is that a yes?"

She nodded. "Yes. With all my heart, yes."

* * *

The twins had no idea how dramatically their lives were about to change, Grant reflected the following morning as he slotted the Lexus into a visitor parking space in front of the apartment building where Janet and the boys lived. He and Janet had decided that all Freddy and Teddy needed to know up front was that Grant would be driving them to church. Otherwise, the whole world would instantly know their news, including half the people on the street, and that wouldn't be fair to Janet's parents.

Hearing that he and Janet were in love and planning to marry would definitely come as a shock, and given Bill's fragile health, they agreed it would be best to break the news gently and diplomatically.

The twins were obviously expecting him because the instant Grant knocked on the door, it flew open and the two little boys hurled themselves at him. It was only by some miracle that he was able to prevent all three of them from crashing into the apartment opposite.

"Whoa, men!" He wrapped an arm around each boy and hugged them close. "I've missed you two! What have you scalawags been up to?"

"Scalawags," Teddy chortled, and tried out the word while Freddy launched into an animated overview of their recent experiences, an account that ended only when his mother made an appearance.

Her soft smile welcomed Grant in a way no words could.

His breath caught in his throat. She was dressed in a simple white wool dress that swirled around her beautiful legs. Her hair was hanging loose on her shoulders in a way that made him long to lose his fingers in it. Or maybe bury his nose in the silky curls and inhale her delicious vanilla scent. Or lift the hair off her neck and brush his lips against the soft skin beneath it.

Or all three...

He limited himself to kissing her with his eyes. "You're beautiful... I love looking at you."

Color rose in her cheeks.

Grant took her hands. "Well?"

She lifted her face to his in a way that came close to destroying what little restraint he had. "Well, what?"

"Have you changed your mind?"

A sheen of moisture made her beautiful brown eyes glisten. "Not a chance, mister."

Grant closed his eyes in relief and took a breath that tested the limits of his dress shirt. More than anything in the world, he wanted to crush her in his arms and kiss her senseless. But this probably wasn't the time, especially with two pairs of six-year-old eyes looking on with an awareness that belied their age. He saw the twins exchange looks of satisfaction and he grinned.

Scalawags...

* * *

Janet felt acutely conspicuous as the four of them filed into Ever Green Community Church and settled in the Caldwell family's customary pew. Her parents arrived soon afterward, and except for Christa's absence, it appeared to be a typical Sunday.

— Until it came time for Children's Church.

The twins, now completely at home with the church programs and staff, and lured by the fact that several of their friends from Ever Green School would also be there, hustled out the moment Children's Church was announced. That left Grant and Janet sitting side by side.

Grant slid closer and immediately linked his fingers with hers.

Janet knew the exact moment her mother noticed. It was right before Pastor Luke's first of three sermon points.

Verna stiffened. Stared. Her eyes moving pointedly from their intertwined fingers to her daughter's face. Janet had no trouble reading the eyes-wide expression that said, *What on earth is going on here?*

Pastor Luke's sermon points were lost to Janet — and quite possibly to her mother, too. She could appreciate her mother having trouble with the fact that she and Grant were holding hands. No doubt Verna still thought of Grant as her other daughter's fiancé. A frank discussion with her parents was definitely in the offing.

Verna appeared uncharacteristically stern as they filed out of the pew at the end of the service and proceeded toward the door. When Grant invited himself for the usual after-church meal, she looked as if she might refuse.

"Janet and I need to talk to you and Bill," Grant said with a confidence and composure than Janet could only admire.

Verna's eyes zoomed down to her daughter's hand,

still snugly enclosed in Grant's. "I should think so," she muttered and marched toward the car.

Grant leaned close. "That went well, don't you think?"

Janet pinched her lips together. "It may take them a while to get used to the idea."

Despite the dampness, Freddy and Teddy set off on their usual sprint around the farmyard the moment Grant brought the SUV to a stop at Ever Green Acres. Janet got out more slowly, in no hurry for the confrontation with her parents. They'd only recently come to forgive her impulsive and irresponsible behavior eight years ago. Would this not strike them as more of the same?

Grant came to her side and slid his arm around her waist. "I meant it when I said I love looking at you." His voice was warm. Intimate.

She managed a tremulous smile.

He gave her waist a little squeeze. "Having second thoughts?"

Janet shook her head.

"You still want to marry me?"

She laid her palm against his cheek and smiled into his eyes. "More than ever."

A relieved grin split Grant's face. He wrapped her in both arms, lifted her off her feet, and swung her in an exuberant circle while planting a kiss on her mouth. "I have to be the happiest man in the world."

"Not half as happy as I am."

He eased her to her feet and pressed his forehead to hers. "Let's go talk to your parents."

Janet left most of the talking to Grant, who very gently and with great sensitivity explained what had taken place. Her father received the news with equanimity; her mother was a harder sell.

"It'll be a terrible blow to Christa, knowing you broke your engagement to her to marry her sister," Verna said.

The twins had no such reservations.

"You mean we're going to marry Uncle Grant?" Freddy asked his mother, the possibility making his brown eyes shine like polished pebbles.

"Can we live in Pop's house?" Teddy wanted to know.

"That," said Grant, "is totally up to your mother."

"I would love to live in Pop's house," Janet declared.

"So would I," said Grant, "so it's settled."

"Yippee!" the twins shrieked and bounced to their chairs at the table.

Janet couldn't muster much of an appetite. Her stomach was a complicated knot of nervousness and anticipation.

Freddy and Teddy, on the other hand, sped through their lunch and ran off to play checkers in the living room. Their grandfather soon excused himself to join them.

That left Janet and Grant with Verna who gave them a calculating look as she scraped what was left of a luscious fruit salad into a smaller bowl. "The two of you seem pretty sure about this. Are you planning to marry soon?"

Grant folded back his shirtsleeves and began stacking the plates. "We haven't discussed that, but the sooner the better, as far as I'm concerned."

Janet felt the same way and said as much.

"It's a shame, really." Verna glanced at them over

her shoulder as she headed for the refrigerator. "We're cancelling one wedding just in time to plan another." She put the bowl inside and closed the door. "Maybe you should think about going ahead with the wedding that's already arranged."

Janet stared at her mother. "You mean Christa's wedding?"

Verna nodded slowly.

Grant hooked an arm around Janet's shoulder. "The idea has merit, Verna, but Janet deserves her own wedding."

"I'm not suggesting she doesn't." Verna's response was crisp, but patient. "But think about it. Everything's arranged. And you have to admit, when Christa plans something, it's planned to perfection."

Janet's laugh was somewhat strained. "That's definitely true. I told Christa she was wasting her talents working in the library. She should hang out her shingle as an event planner." She smiled up at Grant then, and linked her fingers with his where they draped over her shoulder. "Thanks for thinking of me, love."

Verna planted her hands on her hips. "Maybe you should look at the wedding from that perspective, as the work of a professional rather than as Christa's wedding. Think about it. Virtually everything is booked and arranged."

"And paid for," Grant added, then lifted both hands in a gesture that said he regretted speaking so quickly, that he had no desire to influence Janet's decision. "It's totally up to you, sweetheart."

"But the wedding is only ten days away."

Grant slid his arms around her from behind and leaned around to plant a kiss on her cheek. "All the better…"

Verna's eyes were sharp. Going by her expression, Janet guessed the affection she and Grant were displaying so spontaneously was very different from what Verna had witnessed between Grant and Christa. In fact, Janet wondered if Grant ever kissed Christa in anything more than a purely brotherly fashion. Going by what they'd both told her, she doubted it.

And found the thought deeply satisfying.

"If you're as serious as you appear to be," Verna said, "why wait?"

Thanks for no pressure, Mom.

Janet shoved her fingers into her hair. "What about the invitations? People are coming to a wedding where Grant is supposed to be marrying Christa."

Grant turned her to face him. "People are coming to witness the marriage of Bill and Verna Caldwell's daughter. They'll just see a different daughter walking down the aisle." His eyes twinkled. "Think of the excitement that will create. People will talk about our wedding for years to come."

"Oh, goodie. Exactly what I need—another reason for people to gossip about me."

Grant laughed and pulled her into his arms. "I'm only teasing you, sweetheart. But I don't believe anyone would be nasty about it. I predict everyone will think the whole thing is wildly romantic."

Janet hid her face against his chest. "I hope so." Another worry surfaced. "What about the gifts? They've been chosen with you and Christa in mind."

"We can give people the option of taking back their gifts, but I'm betting they won't mind a bit that you're the bride receiving them."

"I agree." Her mother's common sense tone calmed her.

But only temporarily. "What would I wear?"

"Your attendant's dress, of course. The one Christa picked out for you. It's perfect." Her mother's eyes narrowed, as if visualizing Janet in the elegant ivory crepe gown.

It was true. Janet knew she would never find anything more flattering than the sleek, floor-length, ivory silk crepe dress with its lace-edged cap sleeves and deeply draped neckline.

She shook her head to dispel the sense that she'd inadvertently stepped on a madly whirling merry-go-round that was turning too fast for straight thinking. She looked up at Grant. "What do you think?"

"I think we should do as your mom suggests, but the decision is yours, Janet." He pressed a sweet, lingering kiss on her lips. "Only if you're ready."

Oh, she was ready... More than ready. Standing within the circle of Grant's arms, feeling his strength, confident of his love, she knew the answer. It was like he'd said at Pop's house. She'd been waiting all her life for him. "I'm ready."

"Then I say we go for it."

The rest of the afternoon was taken up with wedding plans. Even though Christa had everything organized and in place, there were still some details to consider. Toni would be her bridesmaid. Hallelujah! The ruby red dress was going to come in handy after all.

"What about your groomsman?"

Grant's eyes gleamed wickedly. "I thought I might ask our mutual friend."

"Who on earth would that be?"

"Bart?"

Janet snatched a kitchen towel off the counter and whipped it at him. Grant grabbed the free end and reeled her in. The look in his eye said she was playing with a fire that had no place in her mother's kitchen.

"Be serious."

"The groomsman is a friend of mine. He's a good guy. You'll like him."

She probably would. Janet had no doubt getting to know Grant's friends would be a pleasure.

And as for Bart O'Grady— "I haven't thought about Bart and the money mess in weeks, thanks to you. It's been heaven not having that to worry about."

"I'll do my best to keep it that way. In any case, there's not much to report on that front. My friend tells me there's a forensic audit going on. Bart is cooperating, finally liquidating the assets. That will go a substantial way toward paying his investors. Who knows, if he's willing to shape up, he might even get to keep the company."

Janet was glad to hear Bart was doing the right thing. And even more relieved that chapter of her life was over.

Chapter 22

"**I'm** very happy for you and Grant, dear...but I can't help thinking someone should inform Christa about this turn of events," Verna observed as she checked the line of satin-covered buttons marching down the back of Janet's ivory gown. Her eyes met Janet's in the full-length mirror. They'd had a text from Christa the day she arrived on Grand Bahama Island, but since then, nothing. Not that anyone was anxious about the lack of communication. Christa had made it very clear when she left that she viewed the trip to be an opportunity to 'find herself' and decide what she wanted to do with her life. Janet prayed daily that her sister would find the peace and direction she sought.

She smiled fondly at her mother's reflection. "Christa knows, Mom. Grant sent her a text last night. We thought the news was best coming from him. Christa hasn't answered, but that's okay. She knows."

"I'm glad." Verna continued her inspection, making sure the draped neckline of Janet's gown hung perfectly and that the lace edging on the little capped sleeves was lying straight. "Still, my heart goes out to her." She tucked a wayward cocoa curl into the elegant upsweep held in place by mother-of-pearl combs, then patted her daughter's shoulder. "You look perfect, my dear. And perfectly lovely."

"Mom, you do know that Christa never loved Grant, don't you? She admitted that to me the day I came home." Janet's one-armed hug was careful not to muss

Verna's smart taupe-colored suit. "If God could do this for me, after all my messes and mistakes, I'm positive He has someone wonderful out there for Christa. Someone she'll love as completely as I love Grant."

Verna's smile was not quite steady. "I do hope you're right, dear." She straightened then, and looked toward the bedroom door. "Now let's go see what's happened to that limo."

Thanks to Christa's meticulous planning, pulling together a wedding in only ten days had proven completely do-able. The biggest hurdle was fitting in the marriage preparation sessions Pastor Luke from Ever Green Community Church insisted upon. He was more than accommodating and went out of his way to meet with the two of them almost daily. Grant had already worked through all but the last sessions with Christa. It was a telling moment for Janet when Pastor Luke remarked on the genuine love and commitment he perceived on both their parts.

The only major change Janet made in the pre-arranged wedding was the bride's bouquet. Christa's plan called for a monochromatic color scheme of white/ivory and taupe; her bride's bouquet had featured white roses in a nest of glossy greenery. Janet substituted roses in tones to match Toni's ruby red dress. The rosebud boutonnieres and corsages coordinated, as well.

Distributing the flowers today was Toni's job. Janet could hear her bridesmaid in the living room trying to keep the twins in one place long enough to get a rosebud fixed on their pint-sized tuxedos.

The boys were going to accompany Janet down the aisle, one on either side. She could only hope they'd be appropriately dignified in their behavior, and not try high-fiving every familiar person in the pews along the way. Or jump up and down at the back of the church and yell out, "Look at us!" to the groom waiting at the front with the pastor and groomsman.

The latter scenario seemed a very real possibility when she heard the twins doing jumping jacks in the living room and shouting: "It's coming! It's coming!"

The limo had arrived.

This was it.

She turned to her mother. "Ready, Mom?"

Verna stood for a moment, taking mental inventory, making sure she had everything she might need. "I think I'm ready. What about you?"

Despite her expressions of sympathy for Christa, Verna's eyes held only love and motherly concern for her younger daughter. But Janet knew her mother's question was about more than the immediate. She was asking if Janet was truly ready to commit herself to Grant, this man she'd known for mere months. Janet had no hesitation.

"I'm more than ready, Mom."

"Then come, dear, it's time to go."

They joined the assembly in the living room. Her father, looking handsome in his new charcoal gray suit, looked stronger than she'd seen him since her arrival. Toni was ravishing in her splendid ruby red gown, the hue dramatic against the foil of her sleekly coiled, coal black hair. And the boys— The sight of them in their junior tuxedos brought a lump to her throat...

Any remark she might have made about their appearance was highjacked by Freddy. "Wow, Mommy! Uncle Grant— I mean, our new daddy is *really* gonna love looking at you today!" His face-wide grin revealed an endearing gap where he'd recently lost a tooth.

"Thank you, Freddy. I think that's the nicest thing anyone's ever said to me. You and your brother look pretty spiffy, too."

"Yeah, we know."

Janet and Toni exchanged a look.

Toni leaned close. "He's right, you know. Grant won't be able to take his eyes off you."

The way Toni said it set a shiver of delight and anticipation dancing around in Janet's stomach. Delight that she was marrying the love of her life. Anticipation at the thought of becoming his wife. Giving herself wholly to this man she loved so deeply.

She wasn't exactly sure where they were going for their honeymoon, and hadn't asked. It really didn't matter. Just being with Grant would be enough. He'd hinted at a romantic hideaway on a tropical island. "Pack light," he said, waggling his eyebrows Groucho Marx-style.

The boys were excited about the prospect of spending the time at the farm with their grandparents while she and Grant were away. Janet had made arrangements for the school bus to pick them up at the end of the lane; Toni had promised to be available if Bill and Verna needed a helping hand or a break.

The limo carried them smoothly to the church. Janet breathed a prayer of thanks for the break in the weather. December on Washington State's west coast generally meant rain—or worse. This day was marvelously clear. It was like a special gift.

The parking lot at Ever Green Community Church was comfortably full, a reality that revived the nervous flutterings in Janet's stomach. Much as she'd tried to persuade herself that Grant was right, that ultimately no one would care that she was the bride and not Christa, that they would extend their blessings and good wishes regardless, uncertainty remained.

The limousine pulled up to a side door where the church's wedding coordinator was waiting. She whisked Janet and the boys away to 'the bride's room,' and directed Verna and Bill to the place from which they would be escorted into the sanctuary. Toni hurried off to make sure the rest of the bridal party had their corsages and boutonnieres properly secured.

They had fifteen minutes before the ceremony was scheduled to start. Janet had no plan to be late, one reason being the twins' scarcely controlled energy. The two soon tired of practicing the super-slow aisle walk and had just launched a raucous game of Paper, Rock, Scissors over nothing in particular when the wedding coordinator stuck her head in the door. "Grant's parents just went in," she announced, then withdrew again to her command post.

Grant's mother Maryann and his step-father Tom Forsythe had flown in a couple of days earlier from Palm Springs. They'd welcomed her warmly and were charmed by the twins, delighted at the prospect of becoming instant grandparents.

More reasons for gratitude.

The coordinator returned. "Your parents are seated." She turned to Toni who had slipped in behind her. "It's your turn next, Toni. Janet, you and the boys can come, too. Just stay out of sight until I give the cue."

Janet felt a distinct quickening in her chest as she and the boys trailed Toni to the now-empty foyer.

Thankfully, the solemnity of the occasion seemed to have a subduing effect on the twins. They obligingly took their places, one on either side of their mother, and waited just out of the congregation's sight while Toni made her slow and dignified way up the center aisle to the front.

Once Toni had joined the party on the platform, there were a few seconds of silence before the music changed and the organist began the stately processional music Christa had so capably chosen.

At Pastor Luke's signal, the congregation rose.

Janet used the cover of the music to run through the instructions one more time. "Stay close. Walk slow. And remember, we'll stop at the end of the aisle. When Pastor Luke asks, 'Who gives this woman to marry this man?' what do you say?"

Teddy knew the answer. "'We do.'"

"And you'll both say it at the same time, right?"

"Right."

She could only hope...

Janet straightened. "Okay, then. This is our music."

Teddy grinned up at his mother. "Let's hit the road."

Oh, boy....

"Just stick with me. And remember, walk slowly."

They began their deliberate procession up the aisle. Though Janet kept her eyes fixed on the ornate candelabra on the platform with its chevron of lighted candles, she was aware of double-takes, mouths agape, and audible murmurs. Some even turned around to see if the organist had it wrong and the bride they expected to see had yet to make her appearance.

The boys were getting their share of attention, too. Above the music, she heard several "So cute" and

"Aren't they adorable?" remarks.

Through it all Janet kept moving forward, drawn by Pastor Luke's encouraging smile, the groomsman's look of interest.

And Grant—

Grant, looking heartstoppingly handsome in a classic tuxedo, watched her every movement, the expression on his face sending the butterflies in her abdomen into frantic flight. His look of admiration pulled her like a magnet.

Sudden tears dimmed her vision. She was about to join herself to this man who loved her so completely, so unashamedly. This amazing man God had given her to have and to hold. This wonderful man God had planned all along would become her husband...

The closer she and the boys came to the altar, the wider Grant's smile grew. Her heart sang with joy. He had no regrets. No doubts.

And neither did she.

The boys were doing a remarkable job of controlling themselves, she noticed, though from the corner of her eye she saw Freddy lift one hand close to his chest and wave it at Grant. Even at this distance and through the shimmer of tears, she saw Grant's eyes crinkle at the corners. He lifted his own hand to waist level and waved back at her impish little boy. The tears threatened to spill over.

Thank you, Father... Bless this good, good man. I know he will be the loving father my boys deserve and need.

Three steps more and they were even with the front pew. Janet stopped. The boys halted beside her. Their concentration was almost palpable.

The final strains of the bride's music lingered, then

evaporated into the ether of the sanctuary.

"The congregation may be seated."

Pastor Luke looked out over the crowd, a smile creasing his face.

"God tells us in His Word that He moves in mysterious ways His wonders to perform. What we are witnessing this afternoon is one of those mysterious wonders." He nodded toward Janet. "You've probably noticed that this is not the bride you expected to see coming up the aisle. God, apparently, had a different plan."

He continued to address the gathering. "In the past ten days, I have met a number of times with our good friend Grant Brooks and Janet Caldwell O'Grady for marriage preparation sessions. I want you all to know that the love these two share is deep, and genuine, and real. It is a beautiful picture of the love ordained between a man and a woman by our gracious Heavenly Father. Therefore, I invite you to rejoice with me today as we unite this man and this woman in holy matrimony."

Pastor Luke shifted his stance slightly, as if it were now time to get down to the serious business of marrying. "Who gives this woman to marry this man?"

He looked down at the twins who needed no cue. On either side of their mother, Freddy and Teddy leaned forward slightly, as if to consult each other, then with a quick nod, they declared in voices loud enough to be heard in every corner of the sanctuary—and beyond, "We do!"

Chuckles rippled through the congregation, banishing the atmosphere of tension that had seemed heavy enough to suffocate. Janet could almost feel the mood lightening, and though she couldn't see their faces, she sensed the gathering's acceptance and support for this unexpected change in circumstances. Her heart swelled with emotion.

Thank You, God. You are so good.

Having performed their duty, Freddy and Teddy moved quickly to sit with Bill and Verna, and Grant came down from the platform to claim his bride.

His sea-gray eyes never left hers as he descended the steps and moved toward her.

"You look beautiful," he whispered as he captured her hand in his. Janet could tell he wanted to kiss her, and she thought he might just break with tradition and do that. But after a few charged seconds, he simply smiled, tucked her hand in the crook of his arm and escorted her up to the platform where they took their places in front of Pastor Luke.

Janet fully intended to slide her hand from Grant's arm and wrap it around her bouquet, but Grant had other ideas. He kept it snugly clasped between them as if he never intended to break the contact. Janet wasn't sure this was conventional wedding protocol, but then, nothing much about this wedding was conventional.

And so, with her hand nestled securely in Grant's, she listened to Pastor Luke describe marriage as a picture of Christ's loving relationship with believers, His Church, and what it meant in terms of a man and woman entering into the intimate marriage relationship as she and Grant were doing.

Janet listened, but a part of her mind couldn't help marveling at how God had been at work in her life without her even being aware. He had answered her desperate prayers for help back in Sacramento when everything looked bleak and completely hopeless. She'd gone to Him in dire need, praying for guidance and direction regarding where she could go to start over, to establish a good and nurturing life for her boys. And God had provided. There'd been no light bulb moment, no pulsing billboard message, no Voice rumbling a direct answer, but God had made a way nevertheless.

She'd thought her flight to Ever Green was her own fear-filled response to Bart's threats to her children. In fact, it was a Divine nudge, a part of God's unbelievable plan for her life. And in spite of her mistakes and missteps, He had indeed made a way for her and given her far more than she deserved or could ever have imagined. Gratitude bubbled over in her heart.

When it was time to exchange vows, Janet handed her bouquet to Toni whose eyes were glistening with moisture. She gave Toni's hand a little squeeze. She'd come to love Toni and value her as a dear friend. She hoped with all her heart that Toni would soon find the man God had waiting for her to love, someone as wonderful as Grant.

The wedding ceremony of Christa's planning had included contemporary marriage vows phrased in modern language. Janet and Grant had chosen to share traditional vows, the kind that echoed and reaffirmed promises that had stood the test of generations.

"In the Name of Jesus, I, Janet Elaine, take you, Grant Dawson, to be my husband, to have and to hold from this day forward; for better, for worse; for richer, for poorer; in sickness and in health; to love and to cherish for as long as we both shall live. This is my solemn vow, and I make it with all my heart."

Now holding both her hands in his, Grant voiced the same promises. His thumb caressed the fourth finger of her left hand as he spoke them, the finger that would soon receive his wedding band, the symbol of their as-long-as-we-both-shall-live love.

Grant had offered to buy her a diamond engagement ring, but then he showed her the ring his grandfather had given Gram on their fiftieth wedding anniversary. It was made of fine gold and fitted with a double row of emerald-cut diamonds. Janet fell in love with it immediately and knew Grant was pleased she'd chosen that particular ring to be the one he would slip on her finger to make her his wife. They'd chosen an etched gold band for him.

At the point in the marriage ceremony where she expected Pastor Luke to request the rings from the attendants, he turned instead to Grant.

"And now, do you, Grant, promise to accept Janet's sons, Freddy and Teddy, as your own, to love and nurture them to the best of your ability, and with God's help be a devoted father and a godly example to them?"

Grant's deep voice, that had elicited such a strong response in her the first time they met, now declared with conviction, "I promise, so help me God."

Janet couldn't prevent an emotion-laced gasp. Grant had told her he wanted to adopt her boys as soon as possible, but including this declaration in their service of marriage was a complete surprise. It was a profound and unexpected gift of love.

She couldn't help herself. Protocol be hanged! Lifting her free hand to Grant's cheek, she leaned close and kissed him on the lips. "Thank you," she whispered, the words coming out thick and wobbly.

The spontaneous gesture took Pastor Luke by surprise. "Not yet," he whispered, obviously thinking she had mistaken the cue for the kiss that followed the pronouncement.

"Sorry," Janet murmured.

Thanks to the pastor's lapel mic, the exchange was audible to the entire assembly, and once again chuckles warmed the sanctuary.

Grant didn't look one bit sorry. His voice was still gravelly with emotion when he repeated the time-honored vows a few seconds later, "With this ring I thee wed," and he slid Gram's diamond-studded band on her finger.

"By the power vested in me by God and the State of Washington, I am delighted to pronounce you husband and wife." Pastor Luke grinned at Janet. "*Now* you can kiss him."

Grant wrapped his arms around Janet, almost lifting her off her feet, and kissed her jubilantly. And at that precise moment, a shaft of sunlight through a side window glanced off the burnished brass cross on the back wall and backlit the embracing couple with an explosion of light. Applause erupted from the congregation. People would remark for a long time afterward that it seemed as if God's light had burst forth as an expression of His special blessing on this couple.

When the applause died away, Pastor Luke announced, "Ladies and gentlemen, it is my very great pleasure to present to you for the first time as husband and wife, Grant and Janet Brooks."

The organist launched into a triumphant recessional.

Grant and Janet had scarcely begun their journey down the aisle when the twins dashed up and pressed in between them.

Freddy beamed up at Grant. "Don't forget us."

Teddy had to shout to be heard above the music and the applause. "Are we married now?"

"We certainly are."

Grant caught Janet's eye as the four of them emerged from the church together into brilliant sunlight. The love she saw in his eyes made her heart tumble over itself with joy. Without hesitation, she leaned across the heads of her — no, *their* boys, to meet his kiss.

About the Author

Darlene Polachic has worked as a freelance writer for almost three decades, and has enjoyed a love affair with romantic fiction for much longer than that. She lives with her husband in Saskatchewan, Canada.

Watch for Book Two in her Ever Green Romance Series, *FOR RICHER, FOR POORER,* in the Fall of 2017.

Connect with Darlene on FaceBook
(https://www.facebook.com/darlene.polachic)

www.ingramcontent.com/pod-product-compliance
Lightning Source LLC
Chambersburg PA
CBHW031711170626
46808CB00005B/1702